The Path to True Bliss
Ruth's Journey

BY: DEBORA L. GOWANS

ISBN: 9798319494054

Library of Congress Control Number

Printed in the United States of America

This book is dedicated to my mother, Rutha Mae Gowans, who taught me to have faith and believe that God will make a way.

To my daughters, Rhonda Mitchell, Erika Keyton, and bonus daughter Shannon Glenn, who encouraged and believed in me. Your love and support mean the world to me.

To my sisters, Desiree Gowans, Joyce Thompson, Sheri Spears, and Jackie Joiner. Thank you for keeping me grounded and true to myself.

To my sister/friend
Rev. Minister Reiki Master Sharon Thompson
Thank you for being so very excited for me.

To my dearest friends
Wendy Rose and Dawn Pile Sully
Thank you!

Prologue

The Georgia International Convention Center buzzed with excitement as gifted children from across the city gathered for the Creative Arts Youth Expression Expo. Renowned artists from around the world came to mentor and engage these young talents in exploring and expressing their imagination and emotions through the gift of art. The center housed various rooms dedicated to dance, art, painting, media design, music, singing, drama, and other forms of artistic expression.

In the Canvas Arts Room for 4 to 6-year-olds, Lydia stood before an easel at the back of the room. Her brush moved effortlessly across the canvas, creating a vibrant green forest filled with lush plants and trees. Each stroke of her brush seemed guided with precision and purpose. After Lydia completed the forest, her friend Noah approached the easel as if entranced and began painting a path with soft edges and beautiful flowers. As he finished the last flower, his friend Elijah joined in, adding a soft glow of sunlight that emanated at the end of the path. The trio stood together wordlessly, silently sending prayers for their loved ones. The love radiating from the children was palpable, charging the atmosphere around them.

In a realm beyond time and space, where there were no walls, floors, or ceilings, their voices resonated. The Heavenly Council of Twelve is a divine assembly of twelve exalted beings who serve as the governing force or wisdom keepers of the cosmos. Each member represents a facet of divine order, including justice, mercy, knowledge, creation, time, and others. Seated in a realm beyond time, they convene not with words but with resonances—pure thought and intention shaping the fate of worlds. Their presence is neither authoritarian nor detached; rather, they are guardians of balance, guiding the evolution of souls, the unfolding of prophecy, and the maintenance of harmony across realms. The divine beings, drawn together by the powerful emotions of love, hope, and faith held by the children, gathered in response to their prayers. Holding forth the image of the children and the painting, they observed a multitude of angels adoring and lovingly surrounding them. They summoned Christian, who appeared promptly. Christian, whose very name meant awakening enlightenment, stood with the sword of light that allowed him to cut away the strings of darkness that held people back from their true bliss.

"Behold the call of the children. The three of them have formed the perfect trinity of faith, hope, and love," Christian announced. The twelve began speaking in an ancient, eloquent language, and Christian could feel the energy quickening within him as he disappeared.

The painting began to glow, projecting beams of light from the soft sunlight Elijah had painted. A figure materialized in the painting's glow, growing until it stepped right out of the canvas. The children stepped back, not in fear but in awe, as Christian fully materialized. Sent in response to their prayers, he knelt and drew the three small children to him. With a touch of his hand upon each tiny chest, he eliminated the strings of darkness that tied bands of fear and worry to their hearts. The light erupted from him into each child, and they, too, began glowing with a soft radiance of love. The children moved on to other activities peacefully. At the same time, Christian embarked on his assignments, knowing precisely what he needed to do to fulfill the promise embedded in the children's hearts.

Debora L Gowans

Chapter 1

*Rain showers my spirit
and waters my soul.*
—Emily Logan Decens

Something about a rainy day makes the world seem gray — inside and out. And yet, the thought of stepping out into the pouring rain feels alluring, almost inviting, as if the downpour might wash away all the dirt and grime weighing down my spirit. One more hour on this job, and then I'm out of here — only to head back home to a different kind of work, the kind with no end in sight. "Ruth, daydream on your own time; wait tables on mine," barked Ray, the sole owner and proprietor of the diner where I'd been working from the age of eighteen. This isn't how I pictured my life at thirty-two. I had dreams of building a career in sales and marketing. I had a knack for weaving narratives that drew people in.

I could sell just about anything — and had done so here at Ray's Diner whenever I got the chance. But Ray was one of those men who believed women should be seen, not heard, so convincing him to use my ideas was never easy.

I had always dreamed of going to business school, getting my degree, building a career, and then getting married and having children. Now, all of those dreams were just that: dreams. I couldn't afford college, and I didn't have any extra money—or time. My heart sank as I caught a glimpse of my reflection in the diner window. I looked like death warmed over. My uniform sagged on me like a potato sack. I had never weighed much, and keeping the 105 pounds, I already carried was a challenge in itself. Oh God, I look like I'm forty and hungover. My stringy, lifeless blond hair looked as if I hadn't washed it in over a month.

I looked pitiful. It was days like this—working ten-hour shifts for less than minimum wage—that made me wonder why and how I even bothered to go on.

****

Across the street from the diner, in the deep recesses of a doorway, Christian watched Ruth. He was incorporeal, not seen or heard. He felt the energy of her deep depression suffocating her and obstructing any hope of feeling any real love or joy. He knew the only way to reach her was through love, real, uninhibited love. She had to feel love for herself before she could feel it for anyone else. Christian would give her a little touch of love to plant the seed. The energy swirled around him as he shifted into the shape of a man and crossed the street to enter the diner.

****

I walked over to Table 4, feeling like I was dragging the weight of two worlds on my shoulders. Still, I perked up and flashed my best smile. "The special of the day is turkey meatloaf. You get your choice of two sides, a roll, dessert, and a drink for $9.99!" I announced brightly. As I looked at the customer, I noticed he was a handsome, clean-cut man—definitely not the type we usually got at the diner at this time of day. He finally looked up from the menu, and as he handed it back to me, his fingers brushed against mine.

An explosion of light ignited within me at his touch. His penetrating gaze seemed to reach into my very soul, his blue eyes so deep and piercing that I felt as if I were falling into the endless depths of the ocean. Then he spoke, his voice a soft caress against my heart, his words echoing all around me as if whispered by the universe itself: "You must truly love her first." In a blur of motion, I felt myself transported to another place and time, stripped bare, standing naked before a truth I had long refused to face. Standing before me was a ragged shell of a woman. Her hair was lackluster, her clothing unkept, and her eyes were dead and listless. She appeared to be void of all hope, no longer living life, simply existing. I realized this was me, and I saw myself clearly—fragile and raw—as I understood the impossible was being asked of me: to love her, to love myself. My heart pounded in my chest, and time itself seemed to pause, holding its breath for this moment of truth. I stood bathed in an extraordinary golden light, with soft white feathers floating all around me. I felt weightless, cradled in an immense and unconditional love. Suddenly, the sharp thud of the order pad hitting the floor yanked me back to reality. I watched as he leaned over, smiling brilliantly as he picked up the pad and handed it back to me. "Ruth, I'll have the special with green beans, mashed potatoes, apple pie, and milk," he said warmly. I scribbled down his order, trying to steady myself enough to walk away without collapsing. "Coming right up!" I called, fighting to keep my voice from cracking. What just happened? I wondered, dazed. Maybe I need to get a little more rest. Shaking off the feeling, I rushed the order to the kitchen. "Another special, Ray!" I yelled as I placed the ticket in the window.

I filled a glass with milk and walked back over to the table with the pie, almost drawn back by an unseen force, setting the glass down before the stranger who had just shaken my world with a touch. "What brings you in here?" I asked, curious now to know if he was a tourist or some foodic. Our regular clientele consisted of workers from one of the several construction sites in the area, and he was obviously not a welder or pipefitter. "I had to visit someone special in the area," he said. I noticed an astounding warmth about him that, strangely enough, made me feel comforted, like I was wrapped in a big fluffy blanket. He lit up the room. His smile was genuine, and his voice had a soothing tone that made you want to talk to him all day. I realized that I had been just staring at him, and I finally said, "I'll be right back with the rest of your order."

I turned to walk away. As I finished my shift, I continued watching him out of the corner of my eye. He quietly finished his meal, and as I returned his change from the check, he said, "Thank you, Ruth," as if my name belonged to someone he had always loved with all his heart. I watched as he walked out the door and felt the cold grayness of the day seep back into my world. It didn't take Brenda long to rush over to me to get the scoop on him. "Who was that guy? He was gorgeous! He can put his shoes under my bed anytime!"

****

Christian walked out the diner door and vanished into the grey day. He could see the seed of love taking root inside of Ruth. He knew she would question the entire experience that had shaken her to her core. He would have to show her the truth in a way that would be undeniable.

Chapter 2

"You drown not by falling into the river, but by staying submerged in it".
—*Paulo Coelho*

The only good thing about my job was that it wasn't far from my apartment—if you could even call it that. The Mable Pine Apartments were low-rent units located on Boulevard in Atlanta. My two-bedroom, government-subsidized apartment sat on the third floor of a building that should have been condemned before I was even born. It was a state-assisted Section 8 housing unit that still cost more than it was worth. We didn't qualify for a three-bedroom because the rules required at least two people in every bedroom. Even with food stamps and state aid, I could barely afford to feed and clothe four growing kids.

At just twelve years old, Sara was more mature than I had ever been. She cared for the younger ones—and even for me—when it should have been the other way around. It took every ounce of strength I had to climb the four flights of stairs, and by the time I reached the third-floor landing, I could already smell the spaghetti before even opening the door. Sara had figured out that with a can of peas, a box of spaghetti, a pound of beef, and a jar of store-brand sauce, she could feed our family of five for two days for just over ten dollars. She loved to cook and made dinner every night, thriving on the challenge of combining the little food we had into a real meal. Each week, Sara gave me a grocery list of the ingredients she would need for her planned meals. Not only did she prepare dinners, but she also made desserts and snacks. She had been cooking for us since she was eight years old, and I often thought about signing her up for Master-Chef Junior. While other girls her age were playing, Sara was busy making donuts out of canned biscuits or using a potato peeler to slice potatoes thin enough to fry into homemade chips.

I opened the door and found Lydia and Luke watching TV. Luke jumps up and runs to the door for a hug and kiss. Lydia never even notices I'm there, and Sara comes out from the kitchen to set a couple of bowls on the table. "Luke, Lydia, time to eat," says Sara. "Where's Matt?" I asked. "He said he was going to play basketball," replied Sara. Matt stayed away from the apartment as much as he could, and even when he was there, he didn't have too much to say to anyone, and if he did say something, it was mean and nasty. At 16, Matt was every bit of a teenager. He didn't want anything to do with me or his brother and sisters. He was so hard to figure out, and I never knew what to say or do for him, so we just stayed out of each other's way. It worried me that he spent so much time in the streets. I prayed he would steer clear of the gangs and all the bad influences the streets offered a teenager these days. Matt looked so much like his father did at that age.

His father, I thought to myself, with sad longings of the past —my first love, or at least what I thought was love. I had never known what it felt like to be truly loved before, and no one had ever cared about me until he came along. I was only sixteen, in my junior year of high school, when we met. Mother and I had just moved during Christmas break—the second time in less than a year—and once again, I was the new girl at school. Luckily for me, a new senior named Aaron had also moved into the neighborhood, all the way from California. Aaron still seemed to carry the sun in his eyes—or at least, that's how it felt every time I looked into them. I immediately developed the biggest crush on him.

As an advanced student, I was enrolled in several senior-level classes. Aaron was in my first two classes of the day: Calculus and Physics. The classes were difficult, and we often ended up studying together. Neither of us had made many friends yet, so we spent a lot of time with each other.

At first, it was just schoolwork that brought us together. I never dared to dream he might think of me in any other way—until the day he kissed me. My heart exploded with joy, and our friendship quickly blossomed into romance. My mother was rarely home, and half the time, I wondered if she even knew I existed. When she wasn't working, she was out drinking at the bar. She drifted from one man to another, and we often moved in with someone she had known for only a week—or even less. I was lucky if there was food in the house; more often than not, my only meals were the free breakfast and lunch offered at school. Aaron made me feel special, like finally, someone cared about me. I was young and in love, willing to do anything and everything to show Aaron how much I loved him.

Regarding Aaron, "no" was not in my vocabulary. We spent every possible minute together the first few weeks until baseball practice started. We spent less time together as he became increasingly obsessed with playing on the baseball team.

The time we spent together had gradually turned into just sex. I began to complain and demand more from him. I knew he was torn between baseball and our relationship. The final straw came when he heard rumors that scouts were scouting him. His dream was to play baseball professionally, and he had to give it everything he had — no distractions allowed. By the end of April, we broke up. We had gone into extra innings, but baseball had won. My world fell apart. I wasn't as important to him as I had believed, and that crushed me more deeply than anything ever had. By the time the school year ended, Matt was on his way, and Aaron graduated from high school with a baseball scholarship to the University of California, Los Angeles (UCLA). I never told Aaron I was pregnant. At first, I kept it from him out of anger — he had chosen baseball over me. But when I finally came to my senses and decided to tell him, school was over, and he was already gone.

My mother was furious. She harped at me to go after Aaron's family for child support. I had no idea how to get in touch with him in California, nor did I want to. He left without saying goodbye. He didn't care about me. Why would he care about our baby? After months of arguing with my mother, she told me I had to find my own place and put me out, saying if I was old enough to have a kid, I was old enough to start supporting myself. I lived on the streets unhoused during the summer and then in a shelter for women and children that helped me until I finished high school, got a job as a waitress, and got my first subsidized apartment. That was the beginning of the end. Nothing had ever felt good or right since then, and I had little hope of anything better.

Not long after I moved into my apartment, I met Johnny. Johnny was the opposite of Aaron, with his dark hair and the mischievous glint in his eyes. He was a charmer, always talking a good game and constantly working on new music he believed would be the next big hit. His favorite pastime was smoking weed and strumming his guitar. During the day, Johnny watched Matt while I worked, freeing him up to play at clubs with his band at night. I wasn't in love with Johnny, but we worked well together. I know he sounds like a smooth talker, but he was good to me and Matt, always helping whenever he had something to contribute. After a few months, he moved in.

He needed a place to stay, and I could use all the help I could get. We decided to get married and less than a year later, Sara was born, and soon after came Lydia and Luke. Johnny loved the children and was a good father. But one day, when Luke was just a year old, Johnny didn't come home. A week later, I found out he had died from an overdose of fentanyl-laced weed. The kids were devastated, and it took us a long time to work through our grief and heal from losing him.

Chapter 3

"Nothing is more exhausting than the task that's never started."
— *Gretchen Rubin*

I took a minute to change out of my waitress uniform before returning to the table to eat dinner with the kids. Luke was bursting with excitement over his news of the day, literally bouncing off the walls, the furniture—everything in his path. I had no idea where he found all that energy, but he always had a smile for me, and it warmed my heart. Tomorrow was the first day of school, and he was thrilled to be starting second grade at a new school. One of my regular customers at the diner—a CATHERINE FERGUSON Charter School teacher—had encouraged me to apply for all the kids. Thankfully, they had all been accepted. Their old school had overcrowded classrooms and poor teacher-to-student ratios. It felt like my kids weren't getting a real education because the teachers spent more time managing discipline than teaching lessons. This year, all my kids would attend a school with better ratios and fewer disciplinary problems. I hoped that meant a real shot at a better education. I hadn't been able to afford new uniforms; second-hand would have to do. At least what they did have would be clean. I felt like there was so much left to do. Before I could lie down and sleep, I had to go to the laundromat, iron clothes, and clean the kitchen. Sara would have helped if she could, but the laundromat was too far, and I didn't want her leaving the kids alone. With four kids, if I didn't do laundry every other day, it piled up fast—and they didn't have that much clothing to begin with.

Matt came into the house just before his curfew, walking past me as if I were invisible. "I'm on my way to do laundry.

Take off those clothes so I can wash them," I said. Without a word, he stripped down to his underwear and tossed his dirty clothes into the basket before disappearing into his room and closing the door. I was too tired to argue. Feeling sad, angry, overwhelmed, and disappointed, I picked up the basket and headed out. I wheeled the laundry basket three blocks to the laundromat by sheer force of will. Half the streetlights were out, and the usual unsavory nighttime crowd had taken over—the hookers, drug dealers, mentally ill, and unhoused lingered in every dark alley and corner. I had learned to walk fast, avoid eye contact, and never engage. The laundromat was an oasis in a sea of desolation—brightly lit and clean, with a police officer always patrolling nearby. It was usually packed at this hour with other mothers like me, working one, two, sometimes three jobs, all trying to keep their families afloat. Often, I had to wait for a machine, but tonight I was lucky. Two empty washers' side by side gave me a chance to do both loads at once while keeping an eye on my clothes. The television played old episodes of Star Trek. As a kid, I had loved the original debates between logical Mister Spock and the passionate Doctor McCoy. Later, I became an even bigger fan of The Next Generation's Captain Jean-Luc Picard. The show always carried a lesson—a sermon, almost—that made me feel a little better about life. Tonight's episode struck home. It encouraged me to keep going, even when I felt like giving up. I finished folding the laundry just as the credits rolled and started the walk home. Everyone was in bed by midnight, and finally, so was I.

I pulled the bed out of the sleeper sofa and settled into the thin, worn-out sheets, feeling every ache in my bones—and the sharp springs poking into my back. I pulled the covers over my head, already drifting off even before my eyes closed. Before sleep fully claimed me, I thought about the stranger at the diner. How had he known my name? I hadn't worn a name tag, and I knew I hadn't introduced myself. I'd been too caught up in my own personal pity party. Maybe he overheard someone else say my name.

****

In his incorporeal state, Christian had watched and followed Ruth all evening. He had shadowed her home, giving her little nudges of energy whenever her strength flagged physically and spiritually. He helped her up the stairs, made the smell of spaghetti more enticing, and even made two laundry machines appear to be in use so they would be ready when Ruth arrived. Knowing she would watch Star Trek, Christian queued up the episode where the Enterprise fled from the Borg. When all seemed lost, Guinan's wisdom to Picard—to never give up— would hit home with Ruth. Christian knew how much the lessons from the show meant to her, and tonight's was no different. Later, as she drifted off to sleep, Christian gathered her ethereal spirit and took her with him beyond the veil.

Chapter 4

"I will love the light for it shows me the way,
yet I will endure the darkness because it shows me the stars."
—Og Mandino

Into the Light

The shimmering white light glistened in waves of intensity as far as the eye could see. It was the brightest light I had ever encountered, yet it didn't hurt to look at. These waves flowed like wind-blown, sheer silk curtains with a life of their own. I felt an overwhelming sense of unconditional love and peace, as though I was being lifted and held, tenderly caressed and adored like a small child. A sweet sound, music to my ears, filled the air—though it wasn't music. I couldn't recall ever hearing anything so beautiful, yet it felt familiar. It made me feel as though I had come home. Home—that was it—but not any home I remembered from my life. I felt complete, whole, connected, yet without the heaviness that typically pulled me down. There was a fragrance, not a perfume, not flowers, but a scent so wonderfully indescribable that I couldn't place a name on it, nor did I want to, for a name would somehow diminish its essence. I reveled in the sight, sounds, fragrance, and feelings of it all, just about to lose myself in it, when I heard a voice. I looked around for the source of the voice until I finally grasped, I hadn't heard it outside of me. I didn't hear the words with my ears; he spoke directly to my heart.

His voice beckoned me, and I followed without any effort of my own. I suddenly realized that I knew this voice—it was the blue-eyed man I had met at the diner. Somehow, I knew his

19

name was Christian, and his name meant awakening or enlightenment. His piercing blue eyes penetrated the bright white light as a pinprick of color in the distance. As the eyes moved toward me, they increased in size and intensity. The clarity of his blue eyes gave way to blue skies full of beautiful, vibrantly colored birds of all sizes, singing a tantalizing melody of notes I had never heard before.

Everything around me was alive, vividly moving, and deeply connected. Everything I had seen up until that moment had felt like a dull, monochrome movie in comparison. Before I could finish my thought, he spoke: "Everything around you is alive and moving, and yes, you are connected to everything. It's all a part of you, and you are a part of it all." I grasped the connection in a way I never could have before. It was as though the truth of it all was being revealed to me at that very moment. I knew that even as the wind gently caressed a blade of grass, I would feel that caress as if I were the blade of grass, and the wind was caressing me. We are all ONE. The sun, the wind, the ocean, the plants—everything is of God, made from the very substance of God. I could sense the energy of life moving everywhere. "From your level of understanding, that is the best description for now," he said. "What you are experiencing is the first layer of the veil being pulled back, allowing you to see." "God is everything, everywhere, evenly present. There is no place where God is not. God is All, and All is God. The intensity of God's presence may vary from your perspective, as you will soon see, but the most important thing for you to understand is that God is always fully present." Understanding and absorbing the truth in everything he said was beyond anything I could have comprehended before that moment. I had access to all I ever wanted to know, without even needing to form a thought. It was perfectly incredible.

I began simultaneously seeing scenes from my life playing out all around me, past, present, and future. I understood that I had chosen this life long before being born. The overall course of my life was set before I even came into the world. The details of my life's experience were up to me. My perspective and attitude toward a situation made all the difference in how I reacted and, therefore, what I experienced. I simultaneously experienced what I thought and felt and what everyone around me thought and felt about what I had said and/or done. I felt the joy and pain I caused others to feel. I saw every choice I made and could have made. There were good scenes and scenes I would have rather not experienced more than once. In this place, there was no sense of judgment— toward me, anyone else, or from anyone at all. There was only love —God's love moving through every situation —and it was good, very good.

The most astonishing realization was the truth about thoughts: <u>thoughts were things</u>. I could see myself thinking them and following their path as they developed, gaining energy until they manifested. I also witnessed how I would destroy some of my most extraordinary thoughts and ideas by immediately countering them with contrary thoughts. The destructive thought was like a drop of water rolling down the wick of a candle, extinguishing the flame before it could grow. I came to understand that, more often than not, I wasn't fully present in the moment I was living. It astonished me how thoughts of yesterday and tomorrow overshadowed the present moment. It was as though a distracting haze loomed over everything, preventing me from seeing clearly or fully experiencing the depth of emotion in the moment. As I reflected on each situation, I could trace a thread connecting it back to something I had previously thought about, as though I were creating my world in real-time. It gave me a strange feeling, realizing that I had planted the seeds for every situation in my life, and had a role in the messes I had created. And yet, everything seemed to unfold so perfectly, as if by design. I could see the timelines of events—how they began and intersected with mine. It was awe-inspiring how everything panned out so perfectly. I marveled at the patterns. I noticed that when I experienced a powerful emotion, everything around me seemed to shift, taking on the color of that emotion. Now, this was life in vivid, living color.

Christian lifted me with a thought, and his voice resounded in my heart. Everything around me began to spin. "I will show you, and you will remember these truth principles in your heart and mind."

The most powerful truth principle revealed to me is that every thought I have is a prayer. God, the universe, or any name I might assign—though I now understand that any name is ultimately inadequate—is always listening. I saw a woman before me walking into a room and kneeling in prayer. As she began to pray, the light inside her grew in size and intensity. It expanded beyond her body, merging with a flow of light that I somehow knew represented the light of infinite possibilities. As this scene faded, I saw a man sit down, cross his legs, and hold his hands out, palms up. He began to meditate, and as he did, the light inside him grew, just as it had with the woman. Another scene unfolded: a young girl walked along a nature path as the light within her expanded. Scenes like these, with different people and varied situations, continued to play out, showing individuals from various religions and spiritual practices everywhere, all connecting to the divine source that lives within us. There was no one specific way this had to be done; it was all based on the intent to connect. I could see that prayer and meditation will always increase God's light in me, through me, and as me. Through these practices, all things are possible for the overall good of all concerned.

The time spent in prayer energized the light that radiated from within. I now understand that light is love, and God is love. During these moments, I knew that the light of God and the love of God radiating from within grew and expanded with the time and intensity of prayer. In stark contrast, the moments spent thinking negative thoughts were different. A dark mist would form over the light inside, hindering the expression of God from radiating beyond the core of man. The negative thoughts and dark mist created dis-ease, facilitating self-destruction from the inside out—not just spiritually, but physically. The only thing that seemed to stop, or even reverse, this dark mist was love. It dawned on me it wasn't God who disappeared when He was most needed—it was man who created the blinders to God's presence.

The scenes before me continued to shift, unfolding images of people giving—something, anything—and witnessing how whatever they gave began to grow, change, and multiply before turning back to the giver. I noticed that when I was genuinely grateful for something, I attracted more of what I appreciated. Every time I gave, an outpouring followed, returning more than I had given, in one form or another. Everything I did, every thought I had, brought a shift in the energy surrounding me—a change that might not be immediately visible but would influence things to come. It felt as if each thought I had was a wish granted, free of judgment about what it would bring. This principle, however, was not selective—it applied regardless of whether the giver was offering something good or bad. The multiplication and return happened either way. I watched a man take credit for a younger woman's work, effectively stealing her opportunity for advancement. A year later, he was promoted to a position he couldn't handle and was fired within months for mismanaging funds. This felt like karma, but somehow, the meaning was more direct. Whatever you give will come back to you, bigger and better than what you gave! A flutter of sparkling gold surrounded me, obscuring everything around me, before slowly receding to reveal thousands of people going about their everyday lives. I was astounded by my newfound ability to perceive and understand what was unfolding in each person's life. The people appeared to exist in one of two states of being. The first group seemed to have their energy and power diminished by focusing on the past or the future, while the second group's power and energy grew as they focused with intention on the present moment. Those focused on the present were sharper and more vibrant. Their path was clear and brilliant. The significance of being present was undeniable.

Angry storm clouds moved in across the horizon. In the distance, I saw a small flame, no larger than a match, advancing toward me. Fueled by negativity, the flame grew stronger and more intense as it drew nearer. As it expanded, it consumed everything positive in its path. I saw people standing in judgment of one another, feeding the fire, and destroying relationships. Thoughts of unforgiveness stoked the flames, manifesting within individuals as pain and disease. Egos further enlarged the fire as people mistreated others, believing they were superior. The fire obliterated everything that truly mattered to them. I recognized that our negativity creates our own hell on earth.

The storm cloud moved on, giving way to a bright, sunny day. A large garden stood with every vegetable and fruit you could imagine. People came from all over to fill their baskets, and the field was never depleted. A warehouse with no end in height, width, or depth stood before me, filled with anything and everything you could ever want. Christian said, "This is the infinite storehouse of God. It has an infinite supply to meet all your needs." I grasped there was no lack of supply. There was only a lack of the ability to see the truth. Christian taught me the truth about prayer, meditation, love, fear, supply, reciprocity, thoughts, and being present. These simple yet powerful principles of living govern the experiences we all have during our lifetimes. Like the Ten Commandments on the rock tablets, these principles were seared into my mind and heart. I couldn't forget them if I tried.

I thought about my life as I applied the principles to my life review. I could now see little sparks bursting into new ideas forming within me. Some of the sparks were big and bright. When those sparks hit me, I was consumed with a passion for creating or acting on the new idea. There were times I could view the spark being snuffed out by thoughts of disbelief and doubt that seemed to make all of eternity sad, as if something great would never be fulfilled. I saw clearly the divine spirit embodied in each spark, supplying everything I needed to fulfill my purpose.

Understanding how efficiently and expertly everything came together for my overall good was incredible. I came to understand that God was with me always, but I was not always open to the gifts God offered me. It dawned on me I was most alone when I had closed the door to God, and all the abundant good was there for me to have. I closed myself off to God when I was angry, doubtful, unforgiving, hateful, envious, and all the other negative emotions I often allowed to overwhelm me. God still loved me no matter what I did or how I felt. God always loves me. It was never God that I needed to forgive me. He already had. It was me that needed to forgive me. It wasn't God punishing me. I was punishing myself. It was never God that hated me. I hated myself. How could I not have known how much God loved me all along?

The scenes faded as my ruminations aligned with my present day, but the intense blue sky remained. In the distance, a white, fluffy cloud swirled and danced toward me. The cloud rushed at me, and before I could form a question, I was swept into it at a dizzying speed. When I emerged from the cloud, I realized I had witnessed my life, as though I had lived it fully, embracing the truth principles Christian had shared with me. It was breathtaking. I desperately tried to hold onto every fragment of the experience, but its details faded quickly. The one thought that resonated in my heart and soul was finding a way to live within that version of my life. In an instant, I had witnessed my future from every conceivable angle. Christian began speaking again, saying, "You have been granted a rare and special opportunity to see the life you could live if you begin living according to the truth principles, I just shared with you. This is the abundant life that God desires for you," he continued, outlining it step by step. He guided me down the path to True Bliss. It all made perfect sense.

****

Christian placed her spiritual body upon her physical form and wove the tangible essence of the journey beyond the veil into her very being. He caressed her with a warm ray of sunlight as he gently parted the curtains. Every minute detail, every tiny speck, carried power and meaning. She was about to embark on her journey now, and he would be with her every step of the way—placing people on her path and opening the doors through which all blessings would flow. He couldn't do it all for her; Ruth had to put in the work and meet the energy halfway.

Chapter 5

"The key to success is to focus our conscious mind on things we desire not things we fear."
— *Brian Tracy*

Awakening to Truth

I reluctantly awakened, much like a lover who hesitates to pull away from a tender kiss. I didn't want to return. I didn't want to leave that extraordinary place filled with vivid colors, overflowing love, and peaceful serenity. But no matter how hard I tried to cling to it, the haze of forgetfulness blurred nearly every memory. I couldn't fully recall the vibrant hues or the overwhelming love that had once been so vivid, and worst of all, the loneliness and despair crept back in, more intense than before. The only thing I could recall with clarity, down to the last word, was the truth of the principles Christian had shown me. He had revealed the undeniable truth about God and the deep connection we all share, a revelation that made perfect sense and settled into my mind with total clarity. The specifics of my future remained out of reach, though the feeling of renewed hope had taken root deep within me.

I opened my eyes to see that I was surrounded by radiant beams of sunshine, infused with little specks of dust shimmering in the golden light of sunrise. Lingering between here and there, wanting to stay and hold on, yet feeling my joy, my insight slipping away, and the awareness of being returned. It was the light of a new day, or dare I admit, the beginning of a new dawn, that was so unlike all the days before. I felt different, and despite my despair, hopeful even, in a way, I had not dared to think in a long time. The last time I felt even close to this hopeful was when I met Aaron, Matt's father. At the same time, I was also frightened, wary, and apprehensive. A lone tear lingered on my cheekbone before running down the side of my face and onto my pillow, damp with tears. I had been crying in my sleep, not tears of sadness but joy. Scenes from my dream lay on the periphery of my consciousness as I endeavored to recall. Gradually, the disjointed scenes from my dream trickled into a cohesive thought, knitting together my journey into the light in what might be an impossible journey. It was so real, as frightening as it was awe-inspiring. Although I couldn't remember the details, I fully understood the gravity of what I had been shown. A gasp escaped my lips, and my body shuddered as I sobbed from my realization of the truth. He had shown me the life I had not dared dream of and presented me with the path to a life of true bliss. Did I have the courage to walk it, to take the first step of believing? Did I have a mustard seed of faith to see it through? I sat up in bed, fully awake now, with a few minutes to myself before the kids would start to get up. Pulling back the covers, I sat on the side of the bed feeling a little overwhelmed and realizing the man in my dream was Christian, who I served at the diner yesterday. He took me on the journey in my dreams, told me how I could get there, and told me what I needed to do to bring this vision into reality. The truth principles were seared into my mind. I knew what I needed to do, but I was still a little shaky on how it would work. I was so grateful for this opportunity to make a change, then realized with a smile that gratitude was one of the principles. "Thank you! Christian, wherever you are, whoever you are," I said out loud. "I can make this change, and I know I can do this! I just needed to see if it was possible. I just needed to see a way to make it happen. Thank you for showing me the way! Thank you!" The tears fell again as my heart swelled. In a grandiose effort, I threw my arms out wide to be open and receptive. I opened my arms, opened my heart, and said, "Yes, I believe."

I stood up with a purpose, as if I were standing up for myself for the first time. I felt like God had called me, and my reply was loud and strong! "God, I'm truly ready to do this now. I'm ready to change my life. I'm ready to follow the path you have shown me. I'm ready to be the me I was born into this life to be. I'm not living for my kids. I'm not living for my job. I'm not living for anyone or anything other than the me you bought me in this life to be." That might have sounded contradictory, but I knew beyond a shadow of a doubt if I lived my life to the fullest, my kids would have a fuller life. I would be a better mother and example of my best self. I approached the window and noticed the day so vivid, so clear. Everything seemed clearer than it had ever looked in my life. The day was brighter, and not just because of the rising sun.

Life had more texture—the texture of unseen love and connection. The day was full of life, real life, no longer gray and drab. The color of life was living. I could smell the green of the grass, I could feel the happiness in the blue sky, and the white fluffy clouds made me lighter. Every color was a sensation. The day was infused with a rainbow of hopes and dreams come true. As the sun rose, a bright beam shot out from between the buildings and engulfed me. I felt as if my soul responded in kind with a beam of love reaching out to join the warmth of the sunshine. God woke me up to not only a new day, but God also woke me up to a new me, a new way of being. Thank you, God, for waking me up this morning!

For what might have been the first time in my life, I began praising God and giving thanks, naming each of my blessings one by one. At first, I felt a little awkward—I hadn't prayed in so long. My previous prayers had been full of pleading and begging. But this time, I thanked God for my kids, my job, and even Ray at the diner. I hadn't realized how blessed I truly was until I started calling out each blessing by name. My kids and I were healthy, we had sound minds, and my children were thriving. I had good people in my life. I also realized that there were things I once would have never considered blessings, but now I could see God's hand in everything that had led me to this moment. Somehow, I knew beyond a shadow of a doubt that there were no accidents or coincidences—only God working things together for my highest and greatest good. I concluded my time in prayer with the only prayer I had ever been taught: the Lord's Prayer.

I decided to get moving, noticing that I didn't have my usual morning aches and pains—the kind I normally felt from being on my feet all day at the diner and from the discomfort of the mattress I had been sleeping on. It felt as though someone had revitalized my body, giving me the energy to start my new way of life with the best possible beginning. Just as I folded up the sofa bed, Luke came running out of his room and wrapped his arms around my waist. He looked up at me with the biggest smile and said, "Good morning, Mommy! I had the best dream about you last night. God was hugging you, and you were so happy." I was astonished, so I asked him, "Luke, what else happened in the dream?" He replied, "I only remember you were happy." I was speechless for a few moments. Did he see me in his dream? No, that couldn't be. Maybe it was more than just a dream. Before I could say anything else, Sara called for Luke to brush his teeth. He dashed off—running everywhere was just how he moved. Meanwhile, Lydia emerged slowly from her room, with Sara gently urging her toward the bathroom.

I walked into the kitchen, smiling at the children whose very presence made me happy. As I prepared breakfast and packed their lunches, I made sure they ate something before leaving for the first day of the new school year. I scrambled cheesy eggs, toasted bread, poured each of them a glass of orange juice, and made them sit and eat before they left. I watched them with wonder as they ate. Lydia, always a picky eater, could be difficult to feed, but she loved eggs, and I felt good knowing she'd go to school with a full stomach. After packing their lunches in their new book bags, I walked them to the door. Matt had yet to emerge from his turn in the bathroom.

I hugged the kids individually as they walked through the door and left. To each of them, I said, "I love you more than the sun, the moon, and the stars!" To my surprise, Lydia, who was first out the door, looked at me and said, "I love you more than yogurt." Luke giggled as he threw his arms around me and said, "I love you more than Spiderman." Sara looked at me as if this whole thing was so tediously annoying and said under her breath, "I love you more than pizza." Matt emerged from the bathroom, grabbed a piece of toast, put some eggs on it, and rushed past me, giving me a quick peck on the cheek. When he reached the bottom stairs, he yelled, "I love you more than basketball!" I laughed and marveled at how love lives in us all.

I began cleaning up and getting dressed for work, but without the usual sense of dread. I was grateful to have a job to get up for and go to. I wanted to tell Eilene about Christian and the dream—or vision—or whatever it was. She would probably think I was crazy, or that I was being silly for believing my life could change so suddenly. I didn't care. I wanted to shout to the world about the simple path we can all take to change our lives. I gave my apartment one last look, then closed the door and headed down the stairs to work.

Chapter 6

"When we give cheerfully and accept gratefully, everyone is blessed."
— *Maya Angelou*

I lived in Atlanta's Old Fourth Ward (OFW) on Boulevard. Boulevard, established in the late 1800s, became the pride of Atlanta by the early 1900s. It featured gorgeous homes and lavish lawns, making it one of the city's most desirable places to live. Redevelopment efforts between 1920 and 1930 resulted in multiple apartment buildings. The population of the OFW continued to grow, reaching nearly 22,000 people by the 1960 census. With this growth came an increase in crime, and by 1970, most buildings were boarded up, with the population dropping to just 6,000. In the mid-1970s, Congress passed the Housing and Community Development Act of 1974, which launched the Section 8 subsidy program. Casablanca Windsor began purchasing properties and rehabilitating old apartment buildings to house people qualifying for Section 8. Over time, Casablanca Windsor became infamous as one of the biggest slumlords in the country. Crime and gang activity increased, and community leaders began collaborating with Casablanca Windsor to renovate properties and reduce the number of Section 8 apartments in each building, striving to create a more economically diverse neighborhood. My building, however, had not yet been renovated and remained 100% Section 8. Management did just enough to maintain the apartments above HUD's minimal standards.

I stepped out of my apartment building into what felt like an entirely new world. It's amazing how everything around you transforms when you shift your perspective and attitude. I paused on the sidewalk, taking a moment to simply be present and observe my neighborhood. The chiseled cornerstone revealed that the building was constructed in 1928. My previous view of this date was that the building was outdated and insignificant, but now I could appreciate its charm and historical value. The neighborhood was gradually evolving as older buildings were renovated and new ones rose up. While the grass around our building was tall and untended, a few of the surrounding buildings had been more carefully maintained.

The city was alive, buzzing with energy around me. The streets teemed with people walking briskly, while the steady flow of cars and buses filled the air with noise. Jackhammers roared, tearing into the roads, while cranes moved effortlessly across the skyline. In the distance, ambulance sirens pierced the air, warning of their approach to the nearby hospital. I began my walk to work, fully aware of everything around me. For the first time, I found myself truly seeing the people I passed, making eye contact and offering a sincere smile and a "Good morning". Maybe it was my imagination, but some people seemed to have a darkness around them, as though the light couldn't quite reach them. A few of them moved slowly, with an almost sluggish heaviness, as if some unseen weight was holding them back. As I passed a parking lot, I noticed a man stepping out of his car, his entire presence exuding an incredibly dark energy. He walked briskly across the lot, heading in my direction. A wave of unease washed over me as he passed, and I overheard him mutter a curse about someone being "a boil on the butt of humanity" and needing to get a job. I turned my gaze in the direction he had been looking and saw a man sitting on a piece of cardboard beside a building, apparently homeless. He was disheveled, but there was a soft, radiant light glowing around him. As our eyes met, he smiled warmly, never asking for anything but offering that heartwarming grin. The smile was contagious, and I found my-self smiling back, feeling lighter for it.

As I turned the corner, I was startled by a woman draped in vibrant purple. I blinked several times to ensure I wasn't imagining things. She stood beside a Mercedes-Benz, scanning the street up and down. This wasn't a neighborhood where you'd typically see a Mercedes parked on the curb. Concerned for her, I wondered if she was okay. But she didn't seem worried, which reassured me more than a little. When she spotted me, her face lit up with joy, and she smiled. Her smile warmed my heart. I remembered one of the truth principles about receiving back what you put out, multiplied. Well, my smiles were starting to multiply, and I was eager for more as the day unfolded. This elegant lady was impeccably dressed in a beautiful purple and lavender dress, paired with matching shoes and a purse. Her grey hair was meticulously styled, and her jewelry, while stately, wasn't gaudy. She stood at least six inches taller than me, not surprising given how short I was. I guessed her to be around 65.

As I approached, she greeted me with a cheerful smile. "Good morning! I wonder if you might help an old lady out of a jam?" Of course!" I replied, "How can I assist you? Could I trouble you to use your cell phone to make a call? she asked. "Mine is dead, and I've run out of gas. Once upon a time, there would have been a phone booth on every corner. Now, they're almost nonexistent," she added with a light giggle.

"I don't own a cell phone, but you can use the phone at the diner where I work. It's just around the corner," I said. She took my hand gently and patted it. Her hands were soft and warm, matching her warm, loving spirit perfectly. "Thank you so much! My name's Gladys, by the way," she said. "I'm Ruth," I replied, gently squeezing her hand before letting go.

Gladys continued talking as we walked toward the diner. "My son always tells me to never let my gas tank dip below a quarter and to keep a charger for my phone in the car. He'd be so upset with me," she said with a smile. She didn't seem too concerned that he would be upset. "I believe life is as simple or as complicated as you make it," she said. "The choice is yours. One person might see the same situation as a problem, and for them, it becomes a problem. But the next person could view it as an opportunity and turn it into something that blesses their life. Most people would panic if they got lost and their phone died. But I was glad for the peace and quiet. I thought I was taking a shortcut to avoid the traffic. I was sure I'd run into a gas station before I ran out of gas. Instead of finding a gas station, I've met a wonderful young lady, and now I'm having a lovely morning walk which is exactly what the doctor ordered," Gladys said, giggling again.

"Well, Gladys, you almost made it," I told her. "The gas station is just a block from the diner where I work. It's a small, neighborhood garage with a single bay and one pump. You might have driven right by and missed it—it's a bit on the shabby side. Johnny, the owner, hasn't bothered to update it with bright lights or flashy signage. He's open from 7 a.m. to 7 p.m. and closes for lunch," I explained. "Johnny handles basic auto maintenance, like oil changes, brakes, and tires, all at a fair price. I like to think of him as a hidden gem. The garage has been in his family for three generations, and his son helps him after school every day," I continued. "The only thing he sells, besides his services and gas, is bottled water. He's not interested in turning it into a convenience store, a lottery agent, or anything else— just a simple gas station," I said, laughing.

I went with her to Johnny's Garage, wanting to stay until she was on her way. The bells on the door jingled as we entered the small waiting area and stood by the counter. A minute later, Johnny emerged from the garage and said, "Hi Ruth, what brings you here today? Did you finally get a car? "No, Johnny, not just yet. But when I do, you'll be the first to take a good look at it," I replied, winking. "I came in to see if you could help this beautiful lady. She ran out of gas a couple of blocks from here and needs a can of gas to get back on the road," I said, turning to Gladys. Johnny looked at Gladys and nodded. "I'd be happy to help. You can borrow one of those little red gas cans and fill it up for $30." Gladys reached into her handbag and pulled out her credit card to hand to Johnny. "I'm sorry, ma'am, but our internet is down, which means our credit card machine isn't working. We can only take cash," Johnny said apologetically. Gladys's shoulders slumped. "I don't have any cash," she said quietly. "Gladys, we can still go to the diner and make a phone call," I suggested. "I could really use a cup of coffee and something to eat. Let's go to your diner," Gladys agreed.

I was so impressed with how she turned everything around into something good. We walked the remaining block to the diner. Gladys said, "I'm so happy I'll get a chance to see your diner. I'll be able to visit with you on purpose next time. What do you recommend for breakfast?" she asked. "I love the French Toast and bacon," I replied. "It's just not breakfast without bacon," we said in unison. We both giggled at our response. I opened the door to the diner and situated Gladys in one of my booths. "Do you need time to review the menu, Gladys?" I said as I prepared to get her a menu. "No, Ruth, I'll have the French Toast and Bacon with a coffee," Gladys replied. Ray was busy and didn't see me walk in. I grabbed the phone handset from behind the counter and gave it to her so she could make her call. Ray finally noticed I was there, "So glad you could join us this morning, sunshine," he said. The air around him was light. I knew he was messing with me like he always did. Despite what seemed like a full morning already, I had arrived at work on time.

Eilene said, "Good morning, Ruth. I just seated that gentleman in your section." "Thank you, Eilene!" I replied as I grabbed my apron and order pad, quickly scribbled down Gladys's order, and placed it on the wheel. I then grabbed a couple of coffee mugs and a pot of coffee before heading over to the gentleman's table. "Good morning, sir. My name is Ruth, and I'll be your server today. Would you like a cup of coffee?" Without looking up from his phone, he nodded. "Yes." "Do you know what you would like, or do you need a minute to review the menu?" I asked. "I'll have two eggs over easy, with two pancakes, sausage, and orange juice," he replied, still not glancing up from his phone. "I'll be back in just a minute with your juice," I said, turning to walk away from his booth. I went over to Gladys's table and poured her a cup of coffee. "The AAA people said someone would be here in about 45 minutes—just enough time to enjoy my breakfast!" Gladys said, her voice bubbly, like a schoolgirl getting away with something. I managed to get in a few minutes with Gladys before the AAA truck arrived. "Ruth, everything happens for a reason. Today, the reason was that I had a wonderful walk and met a beautiful soul named Ruth. Thank you for everything. Have a blessed day!"

Chapter 7

"Normality wasn't in the days I'd left behind me: it was only to be found in whatever fortune placed in my path each morning."
—*Maria Duenas*

As the kids were getting ready for school the next day, Luke spilled juice all down on his shirt. It was his only clean shirt, so I had to take it off him and wash out the stain before drying it with a blow dryer. I didn't want him to hold up the other kids, so I told them I would take him to school. As I signed Luke in, the Principal, Mrs. Collins, walked by, and Luke—ever bubbly and with no topic off-limits—decided to tell her about our morning and why he was late. She listened attentively, then told Luke how happy she was that he made it to school after such an eventful morning. The admin lady gave Luke a pass to take to his teacher and told him he could head to class. Mrs. Collins smiled as he quickly walked to his class, then looked at me and asked, "Ms. McInnis, would you come with me?" She led me into a small room with a large box of lost children's uniforms. "Ms. McInnis, this box contains lost uniform clothing from last year. Please take a few minutes to look through it and take whatever you think you can use. We usually send out an email at the beginning of each year asking parents for their child's sizes and the items they need. We bag up the requested items and distribute them to the families who made requests. As you can see, we still have many leftovers, so please take all you want," Mrs. Collins explained. "Thank you so much," I replied. I thought to myself how, at one point in my life, I might have been offended or embarrassed, but today, I was grateful. Not only did I get several shirts for Luke and Lydia, but I also found pants, gym shorts, and sweaters. Some items even looked better than the clothes I bought from the secondhand store.

I was half an hour late when I finally entered the diner. Ray was yelling at me before I even opened the door. "You're late! You've got two tables waiting for you to grace them with your presence. That is, if you think we could bother you to take their order." Eilene walked by and said, "I got them some water and menus. They don't seem bothered by it." I apologized to Ray, expecting to see him surrounded by dark clouds of anger, only to be amazed that he was bathed in a blissful glow of joy. It was then I understood how much Ray loved this diner. It was never just a job for him. This was his baby, and he was happiest during rush hour.

The diner was a remnant from the fifties, retrofitted with red and white booths and barstools. When you entered, the hostess stand was to your left, and the bar was immediately in front of you. Behind the bar was a beverage counter with the coffee machine, soda fountain, juice machine, and a refrigerator for milk and bottled drinks. In the middle of the counter was the pass-through window to the kitchen, complete with an order wheel. Ray was a big guy who loved looking through the serving window to watch what was happening in the diner. He stood about 6'3" and weighed 270 pounds, filling the entire window when he was in it. His voice was deep and loud, making it easy to hear him from anywhere in the diner when he called you. At 67, his hair was all gray, and he kept a buzz cut—likely a way of holding on to his military days. A retired Marine Corps Gunnery Sergeant, he was proud to share this with anyone who asked. Not a day passed without one or more of his Marine Corps buddies coming into the diner.

Ray's Diner was my first job, and Ray was my only boss. He intimidated me initially with his gruff exterior, but soon he became more like a father to me—and a grandfather to my children. After Johnny died, the kids often came to the diner with me, sitting in a booth to color or do homework. Ray would offer minor complaints, but it was more bark than bite. He spoiled them with cookies and played with them. We spent all our holidays at the diner, and Ray always made them special. They didn't come as often now that I was comfortable leaving them home alone, but the bond between Ray and the kids remained strong.

The diner had an excellent reputation and a loyal customer base, which meant it was usually busy. It was especially popular not just in the metro Atlanta area but across the country, particularly after being featured on a show highlighting diners across America. As I tied my apron and took a deep, cleansing breath, I thought about the lessons from the other night's journey, especially the importance of setting my intention for the day. I took a moment to be still and said, "Today, I will be present. Today, I will be patient. Today, I will be kind. Today, I will stay focused." By lunch, I had earned more tips in the first three hours than I usually made in two days. Later in the afternoon, a man we called Slimy Simon sauntered into the diner. He was always rude and mean. Gathering my resolve, I made it a point to see him through the eyes of love and let go of whatever he had said or done to me in the past. This was, after all, a new day.

"Good afternoon, Simon. What can I get for you today? The special is – "" You know what I want," he growled, "I always get the same thing. Now get my cheeseburger with fries. And take your Mary Poppins smile with you!"

I wrote down his order as I felt his words hit me like a ton of bricks, hurting me deep down to my core. I was beginning to get angry when I remembered something from my vision the night before about hurting people and how they projected the pain they were feeling to others. Instead of receiving the pain he was projecting, I reached deep into my soul for love and felt grateful for having the opportunity to show Simon love when he needed it most. I smiled again as Simon glared at me and said, "Thank you, Simon." He grumbled a little more, but as I glanced back at him, something in his eyes had changed slightly. For a moment, I thought I had broken through the shroud of shadow that clung to him, letting in the faintest glimmer of light—fragile, but real.

When the day was finally over, I left work still feeling energetic. It was still a beautiful day, and I couldn't wait to get home and be with my kids. But as I turned the corner onto my street, I sensed someone following me. He wore a hoodie with shades so that I couldn't see his face. He seemed to be surrounded by a darkness that frightened me. I walked a little faster and thought about how I had learned in my vision that fear is not real. Only love is real. I imagined myself surrounded by the light of God's love and protection. My heart rate and walking pace slowed. I didn't see the guy anymore.

Thankfully, he was gone. I reached my apartment building and saw Matt on the steps with his friends, holding his basketball. As I walked up the stairs, I smelled marijuana smoke. I didn't see any smoke, joints, or roaches on the ground, but I still asked Matt to come inside for a minute. When I closed the door, I asked him if he had been smoking. He quickly denied it. I wanted to believe him, but it was becoming harder every day to even know who he really was. Avoiding an argument, I said it was time for dinner, and we both went upstairs.

When I walked into the apartment, Sara was putting a wet rag on Luke's nose, which was dripping blood. "What happened?" I asked, trying to keep the panic out of my voice. "Luke decided to play baseball with the kids in the neighborhood and tried to hit the ball with his face," Sara said. "I'm fine, Mom. I had so much fun playing," Luke insisted. Nothing ever brought him down, not even a bloody nose.

Matt walked in right behind me, carrying his companion—the basketball. Ignoring Luke, he said, "I'm going to try out for the school team this year. I think I have a good shot. Coach says I could use some work on my defense, but he thinks I'll make a fine player if I put in the effort."

It never ceased to amaze me how adaptable kids could be. Or so I thought, until I looked at Lydia over in the corner, pouting. "What's the matter?" I asked. "They won't let me play with them," Lydia cried. "Who?" I asked. "The girls at school. They said I looked like a homeless kid." Sara spoke up, mentioning that the girls in her class weren't much better. I pulled out the clothes I had gathered from the lost and found box, which helped Luke and Lydia, but I knew Sara still needed new clothes. When I looked at how threadbare their clothes were, I knew the girls had a point.

I had bought most of their clothes secondhand. Come to think of it, I don't think I'd ever bought them new clothes. It didn't matter at the old school because half the kids there looked the same way, and some didn't even have socks to wear. But that wouldn't cut it at this new school. I promised them that everyone would get one new outfit with my next paycheck.

"Lydia, I know you don't understand this now, but you will in the future. Clothes don't make the person; it's the person who makes the clothes. A person can wear a million-dollar outfit, but nothing will make them look good if they're rotten inside. These girls aren't the kind of girls you want to hang out with anyway. If they'll judge you by your clothes, you don't need them. Find some other girls to be friends with. Be the popular girls to each other." At that, Lydia started to giggle. I was happy to see Lydia smile, and so was Sara. Being a child today is hard—though not much easier when I was a little girl. Girls can be treacherous.

We had a nice dinner together, and everyone talked about their good and not-so-good days. By the end of dinner, we decided to play a family game. Matt wanted to play basketball, so I played with the little ones after they finished their homework. Sara usually supervised their homework when she came home, and by the time I could help, it was just a review. Secretly, I was glad because Sara was far more intelligent than I was at that age.

It was late when we finished our third round of Uno. Luke was first in the tub. After he got out, I cleaned it before Lydia bathed. Luke was always quick to get out, and so dirty that he left a ring. Lydia, on the other hand, loved to linger. They put on their pajamas and got in bed to read before going to sleep. Sara preferred to shower in the morning and enjoyed being in her room alone while Lydia was in the tub.

I heard Matt finally come in as I finished reading a story to Luke. I was walking out the door of Luke's room and turned off the lights so he would go to sleep, when I decided to have a little chat with Matt. Looking up at Matt, I said, "Hey, I want to talk to you for a minute." "What's up?" Matt asked. "How are you doing with all these changes?" I asked. "It's all good, Mom. I like my school, and the kids are dope. I met some people and found some good ones to play ball. It's all good," Matt responded.

"Matt, I've been wondering. Have you ever thought much about your father?" I asked. "Not as much as I used to when I was little. You kept it low-key, so I figured he ghosted me. If he doesn't want me, then I don't need or want him," Matt said, suddenly seeming bothered. "Why are you asking me this?" "Well, because you're at a new school, with more kids who have both parents, unlike your old school," I said defensively.

"Kids live without fathers all the time," he said. "I'm good."

"Okay," I said, and he got up and kissed me good night. I wondered how he would take it when (and if) I ever told him about his father. With today's technology and the abundance of information on the Internet, he could probably find Aaron. He may have already looked. He might blame me for not having a relationship with his father. He could hate me. I recognized, though, that thinking the worst wouldn't help anything. Even though I had all the information I needed to walk the path to true bliss, there would still be challenges every day. If I were going to succeed, it would be up to me.

Maintaining an attitude of gratitude and seeing everything through the eyes of love required staying tuned in to what I was thinking and feeling. Slipping into despair was easy if I allowed myself to wallow in the dirty bathwater. I told Lydia to let the sad part of her day go down the drain with her bathwater when she was almost finished. It was time to get out of the funk. No more wallowing in the dirty water from the tub.

Chapter 8

"Then the LORD *answered me and said: "Write the vision And make it plain on tablets, That he may run who reads it."*
—*Habakkuk 2:2*

The children had made it through the first few days at Catherine Ferguson Charter School, and I decided to do a quick load of laundry because Sara was going on a field trip and needed a clean uniform skirt. Walking back from the laundromat, I noticed the man who had followed me home from the diner. He was standing across the street, watching me. Chills ran up my spine, but instead of fear, I envisioned myself surrounded by light and love. Who is this guy? Why is he watching me? I wondered as I raced home. I couldn't call the police because he hadn't done anything wrong. I didn't want to dwell on it. According to my vision from the other night, whatever I focused on would increase. I decided to focus on feeling safe and protected as I lay down and drifted to sleep.

When I woke up in the morning, I still felt that wonderful sense of peace. I decided to start a journal. After the kids left for school, I found one of their old, half-used composition notebooks. I tore out the pages with writing on them and created three columns on the first page. In the first column, I wrote about something from the past for which I was grateful. In the second column, I wrote about the things I was thankful for today, in the present moment. In the third column, I left it blank. Instead, I found a picture of a woman sitting at a desk in an office. She looked happy and had a job she loved. I posted the image over the third column and said aloud: "This or something better is happening for me in my life! Thank you, God!"

In my vision, I remembered how important it is to see what you desire, write it down, and hold on to that vision. I wanted a better job to provide a better life for my kids. Deep in my soul, I knew it was possible, even though I couldn't see how it would happen. I accepted that how it would happen wasn't up to me it was for God to handle. I needed to be ready to receive my good, whenever and wherever it may appear.

As I walked to work, feeling uplifted, I noticed the same guy following me. I refused to be afraid. Instead, I focused on the power of God's love and protection. I noticed that his presence didn't bother me at all anymore. Streets that were usually empty now always seemed to have someone walking near me or across from me. I felt protected.

One day, while serving a customer, an article she was reading about the benefits of meditation caught my attention. She noticed I was interested and shared how meditation had significantly impacted her life. She explained the basics of finding a quiet spot and being still. "Just listen to the air going in and out of your lungs to begin with," she said, handing me the magazine, which she left along with a generous tip.

Later, during my break, I read two helpful articles. The first was about the Prayer of Protection by James Dillet Freeman of Unity. He had written a similar prayer for a Christmas service and later adapted it for a protection pamphlet.

The Prayer of Protection by James Dillet Freeman

The light of God surrounds us
The love of God enfolds us
The power of God protects us
The presence of God watches over us
Wherever we are, God is!

Reading this article warmed my heart. I knew I would memorize this prayer, which would serve as a source of comfort for the rest of my life. The second article discussed using meditation to manifest your desires. It articulated the aspects of my vision that demonstrated how we attract what we most deeply desire. Although I had never tried meditation before, the instructions seemed straightforward. I decided to try it for five minutes before bed and again for five minutes in the morning after journaling. During the first week, I struggled to remain still for just five minutes. But by the middle of the second week, I found it easier to stay still for longer periods. After the third week, I began to notice a real difference. The meditation helped me maintain focus throughout the day, and I gained more clarity of thought.

After a month of journaling and meditating, I began to see my life—and myself—in a new light. I felt more positive about myself, my situation, and my future. I went to work eager to see my coworkers, regular customers, and to meet new ones. Instead of dragging myself up the stairs after work, I walked with a sense of happy anticipation, knowing I'd be greeted with love, hugs, and kisses from my children. On the surface, it didn't seem like any physical change had occurred, but I knew that, for me, it was a whole new world.

Chapter 9

"Prayer should be the key of the day and the lock of the night."
—*George Herbert*

It was the last Friday of September, and the fall colors—orange and red—painted the trees. Pumpkin spice lattes were the hot item on the menu. The Atlanta weather was finally beginning to cool down, offering us a much-needed reprieve from the summer's scorching heat. I felt exuberant as I wrapped up a very lucrative day at the diner. The tips had been incredible, even surpassing the usual amount in several cases. I had reached a point where I finally had some money left after paying my bills.

Just as I was getting ready to leave, Ray called me into his office. I didn't know what to think, as this was highly unusual. He looked troubled as he gestured for me to take a seat. Instead of sitting behind his desk, he sat beside me.

"Ruth, I'm closing the diner," he said. "As much as I love this place, I have to stop working. I've been diagnosed with ALS."

I was in utter shock. I didn't know what to say. Why hadn't I noticed any symptoms? My friend and neighbor, Mr. Moses Powell, had died from ALS a few years ago, so I knew all too well what this diagnosis meant.

I threw my arms around Ray as tears streamed down my face. After a minute, he pulled away, dried my eyes, and tried to lighten the mood by joking that he wasn't dead yet. He went on to talk about how he wanted to take advantage of the time he had left to travel and do all the things he had been putting off for years.

"I'll sell the diner and give each of you a small severance package," Ray said. "Hopefully, it will tide you over until you find a new job. I wanted to tell you all before I put it on the market, so you don't hear it from someone else. I plan to shut the place down in thirty days."

I asked, "Who will take care of you when you can't take care of yourself?" "I know my boyish good looks can be deceiving, but I'm almost seventy," Ray said with a smile. "I'm a retired Marine and civil servant, so I've got a good retirement and social security. I found a skilled nursing facility I like, and I'll move in there when the time comes. No need to worry about me. I've got everything planned out. I don't want to be a burden to anyone. But it would be nice if you and the kids came to visit me. Studies show that people with visitors get better care than those without."

I smiled. Ray always shared tidbits of knowledge he picked up from articles in medical or science magazines—or even The Atlanta Journal-Constitution.

"How did this diagnosis come about?" I asked. "I haven't noticed you having any issues."

"I started having trouble raising my arms to pull orders from the wheel," Ray explained. "It reminded me of how things started for my uncle, so I talked to my doctor. There isn't any test specifically for ALS, but we ran all the tests we could to rule out other causes."

I felt comforted knowing Ray had a plan, but I was also deeply saddened by what he was about to face. Ray had no close family. His wife had passed from cancer before I met him, and his son had died in a car accident a few years ago. He had always considered us here at the diner his family.

"Does anyone else know yet?" I asked.

"You're the last to know," he replied. The tears started up again, and he hugged me tightly. "Ruth, I've lived a good life. No regrets. I'll live it to the fullest until I can't anymore. I'm going to take it one day at a time. I'm going to visit Machu Picchu, see the sunrise over the desert in a hot air balloon, spend time lounging on the beach in Bora Bora, and, lastly, I'll go to Disney World!"

He laughed. "Eileen is going to do some of the traveling with me, and I'd love it if you and the kids would join me for Disney World." My heart melted. "Of course! You say the word, and we're there. The kids will love it."

After we talked, and when I finally stopped crying, I gathered my things and reluctantly left Ray's office to head home. As I walked, it occurred to me that I would soon be out of a job. I had been doing my best to live by the truth principles I'd learned from my vision, but now it seemed things were headed in the wrong direction. I had visualized a better job, not no job. For a moment, I felt discouraged but quickly pushed it aside. I would stick to my routine: praying, meditating, visualizing, and journaling. I would stay in the flow of positive thoughts and energy. I had to believe and keep the faith. God promised it would happen—all I had to do was believe, regardless of how things appeared.

****

Christian watched from the shadows in the deep recesses of the diner as Ruth faced the first blow that would rattle her entire world. Everything she had known was about to change. She had come a long way, and now she would need to dive deeper into faith and belief to not only love herself but to feel worthy of the love others wanted to give her.

As he began praying in an ancient language, a swirl of energy formed a ball in his hands. He gently blew half of it into her heart. She would need this strength for what was coming next. Across town, he blew the other half into the heart of a young man who had long lost his faith. It was time for this man's heart to awaken and recognize the gift that was about to come his way.

Chapter 10

"And that is how change happens. One gesture. One person. One moment at a time."
— *Libba Bray*

The atmosphere at the diner when I returned to work on Monday was somber. Each of us was processing our grief over losing Ray and, by extension, our family. We were a family, and we were losing not only our patriarch and the family home but also our jobs. Over the weekend, I had time to put it all into perspective and use the information I had learned from my vision to find a way to see the good in it all—and that wasn't easy. There was a knowing, without being told, that we are infinite beings and that our time on Earth is but a blink of an eye. I could see in the vision that everything happening to us and around us is for the greater good of all involved.

Death had always felt so final before the vision, but now I knew it was a departure from the physical to the pure spiritual form. Knowing Ray would always be with me gave me some relief, but continuing my life without his physical presence was the true challenge. Then, on top of processing the loss of Ray, I had to also process the loss of my second home and family. Knowing I would no longer be spending my days with the people I had come to love and spent almost every day with for the past ten-plus years was nearly too much to handle. I had no doubt we'd stay in touch as much as possible, but people get busy with everyday life and often put time spent with loved ones on the back burner. Last but certainly not least was losing my job. I was finally making decent money at the diner, and now I would have to start all over. I couldn't complain, considering I had been working on manifesting a new job. I just didn't think it would happen like this. There's an old saying based on Aesop's Fable that says, "Be careful what you ask for, you might just get it," and I was feeling all of that now. Maybe this was God giving me the push I needed to get out of my comfort zone. I had been doing the vision work, journaling, and affirmations for the new job, but I hadn't taken any additional steps to help it manifest. It was time to get to work write a résumé, look at the want ads, apply for jobs, and pay attention to job openings. The path was being forged for new beginnings. It was time to walk it.

Ray was late coming into the diner. I was surprised he showed up at all, considering everything he had to deal with. When he finally arrived, he was with a real estate agent who took pictures of the diner and placed the "For Sale" sign in the window next to the open sign. Ray had bought the diner just before the revitalization project started in this part of town. It had been a foreclosure, so he bought it for the back taxes at auction. The first couple of years were slow until the neighborhood construction started. It only took a few construction crews to sample Ray's food for word to get out. Fifteen years later, the diner had become a neighborhood jewel. This was now a prime location, and Ray had been approached several times in the past with offers. By the end of the day, he had three offers in hand and finally settled on a cash offer that was 30% above his asking price. The closing would take place in the first week of October. It was all happening so fast.

I went to the library over the weekend to use the computer and start looking through the want ads for other restaurants in need of servers, submitting applications as I went. I also applied for a few receptionist jobs, although I didn't have any of the required experience most of them asked for. I would find a new job—I had to, for my kids. There were plenty of waitressing jobs available, but most of them required nights and weekends, meaning I'd have to leave my kids unsupervised more than I already did. I had to keep searching for the right fit, and I believed that it, too, was searching for me.

Trips to the library every evening after dinner, looking for jobs online and in the newspaper, became a part of my daily routine. My heart ached as anxiety grew over finding a job. I'd been on five interviews for waitressing positions, but everyone was for nights and weekends, even at McDonald's. Why was this so difficult? What else could I do to make money? Outside of my high school diploma, I didn't have any skills other than being a mother and a waitress. My self-esteem began to falter. I needed to stand in a place of power and shake off this victim mentality— it was no good for anything. I remembered hearing about the "Superman position" and how it could make you feel powerful and in control. So, I shook my head, stuck out my chest, placed my hands on my hips, and told myself to snap out of it—things would work out. I looked up, blinking back the tears that threatened to fall, and whispered, "Thank you, God."

I knew this was undoubtedly the time to put everything I had learned—and now believed—about manifesting into practice. I began using a technique I had read about, which involved closing your eyes and picturing yourself in a movie theater. The curtains open, and the screen comes to life, showing me doing the work I desired to do. The imagery included the color of the walls, the size and shape of the desk, a computer on the desk, and every other little detail to make the movie as vivid as possible. I understood the importance of feeling myself in that office, dressed for success, and experiencing the excitement associated with my new role. I did this every day alongside my regular meditation practice. I could feel the change within me—my thinking and the application of these truth principles had transformed my life. I had to believe that the excellent job I was visualizing was already mine.

Chapter 11

"If you want something you've never had, you must be willing to do something you've never done."
—*Thomas Jefferson*

It was the last week the diner would be open. The air was charged with an energy of excited anticipation for the new journeys we were all about to begin. Eileen and Ray eagerly looked forward to their travels, constantly huddled over pamphlets outlining the highlights of every city they planned to visit. Brenda was excited to move to Ohio to live with her daughter and grandchildren. Brenda's daughter had just accepted a new position that required her to travel for work, so she needed someone to help her husband with the kids when she was away. Everyone had a plan—except me. I had received some job offers, but none of them felt like the right fit.

On Wednesday, a group of businessmen came in and were engaged in an intense discussion when I approached their table to take their order. "Good afternoon, gentlemen. My name is Ruth, and I'll be your server today," I said. "Can I start by getting you something to drink while you review your menu?" After a brief pause, two ordered coffee, and the other two wanted iced tea. They returned to their discussion, each eager to make his point. I brought their drinks and started describing the specials, highlighting the last lunch special Ray would promote in the diner. Ray always gave us a sample plate of the specials if it was something new, so we could describe it to the customers.

Both lunch specials were fantastic. He called them his "goodbye plates." I gave them my best mouth-watering and appetizing description of the specials. "Gentlemen, you are in for a real treat! Our specials are Neptune's Chicken: two tender, juicy chicken breasts stuffed with Ray's award-winning seafood stuffing, topped with mozzarella cheese and broccoli, with your choice of one of our delicious sides and a roll. Our second special is the Positano Chicken: a perfectly grilled chicken breast sautéed with lemon, garden-fresh basil, and oregano, served over penne pasta with our farm-fresh vegetable medley." I paused and asked, "Do you have any questions?" They all stared at me as if I were from another planet. I'm used to people taking their time to decide, some even changing their minds a few times, but no one had ever just stopped and stared at me like this—let alone four men. I wondered if I had said something wrong or offended them when the youngest-looking guy in the group turned to the others and said, "She is exactly what we need. She has the smile, the passion, and the energy we're looking for as the face of first impressions. She'd be great!"

"Mike, I agree with you," said the older gentleman in the far corner. "I know we all see it, but we've been interviewing people for a week now—people with experience. You don't even know if she wants to do this kind of work, right?" "Look, Jack, I know this is way outside the norm, but she has everything we've been looking for. We need to move quickly before we end up with no one at the front door. It'll take forever if we leave it to HR to find the right candidate. You know how slow they move."

I looked around, trying to figure out who they were talking about. "Would you like me to come back later?" I asked, sensing they had something more important to discuss. "I'll give you some more time to look at the menu, and I'll be back in a few minutes," I said. I turned to walk away when the first gentleman in the opposite corner stopped me in my tracks.

"Wait," he said. "Would you be interested in interviewing for a job with our team?" "Me?" I asked, surprised. "I have to be upfront—I've been doing this all my life," I said with a slight laugh. "What kind of job is this?" "The title is 'Director of First Impressions,'" Mike explained. "In other words, we need a receptionist. Don't worry, we'll train you—we prefer it that way, so you don't have any bad habits to break." "Do you want my resume?" I asked.

Jack looked at me and said, "You just demonstrated the skill set that matters most to us, and as far as I'm concerned, the interview is over. The job is yours if you want it. I don't know exactly how much the pay will be, but I do know the company offers great benefits and an annual bonus."

I was stunned, and I felt my knees begin to buckle beneath me. They had just offered me a job as a receptionist, sitting at a desk! It felt as if the Universe had conspired to bring everything together for this moment. The atmosphere seemed to crackle with energy, so much so that I could almost see the sparks. "You're not teasing me, are you?" I asked, incredulously.

Jack laughed. "No, we truly need someone to fill this position. We run an advertising company, and it's crucial to have the right person greeting our clients and potential customers when they enter the office. We learned the hard way that you can't just put anyone at the front door and expect people to want to walk in after an initial introduction from a rude, unappealing receptionist. Our reputation isn't always enough—people come to our office to see if we're the right fit for them. Your attitude and energy are exactly what we need to set the tone for our customers. And so, Director of First Impressions!"

I was overwhelmed and speechless. "Please say yes," Mike urged. For the first time, I noticed how incredibly handsome he was, and his smile was bright and sincere. "As an added incentive, we can arrange a small sign-on bonus. We offer it to most of our new hires, so I don't see why we couldn't extend the same offer to you," Mike added. "I agree," said Jack. "So, what's your answer?"

"Yes! Yes! I'll take it!" I exclaimed.

People started looking around, but at that point, I couldn't contain my excitement if I tried. "When do you want me to start?" "I'd like you to start as soon as possible," Jack said. "But we'll need to send you to HR to complete some paperwork, undergo a background check, and go through the usual pre-hire procedures to get you on the payroll. Can you come by the office tomorrow? We'll get everything sorted, and I believe we can have you start next week, if that's not too soon." "Well, you gentlemen have certainly made my day," I chirped.

"Ruth!" Ray called from over the grill. "Your order's up! You've got more than one table today—how about spreading some of that love around?" "Okay! Okay! I'm coming!" I yelled back at Ray, then turned to Jack, temporarily at a loss for words.

"Now that we've solved that problem, gentlemen, let's order some lunch," Mike said. "I'll have the Neptune Chicken," Jack said, handing me back the menu. All four ordered the specials.

"I'll be right back with your orders," I said as I turned to walk away. Inside, I was kicking up my heels, overjoyed. I took care of my other tables and brought the orders to Mike and his colleagues as soon as they were ready.

"We've offered you a job, and you don't even know our names," Mike said. "Let me introduce myself. I'm Mike Bradford, and this is Jack Perry, Ron Ericson, and Clarence Simmons. We all work at B&D Media Group." "It's truly a pleasure to meet you all," I said. "My name is Ruth McInnis. I hope you enjoy your meal. I'll be back to check on you."

I walked over to the pick-up window, dazed and shocked. What in the world had just happened? My life was about to change in a big way. Was this the opportunity I'd been dreaming of? The chance to live a different life?

Before long, Mike called for the check, and they left, leaving me a business card and a generous tip. He smiled and said he'd see me tomorrow as he walked out the door. It took all my will-power not to cry. My life was finally about to begin anew. I was on the path to the life I had always wanted.

Chapter 12

"Sometimes we're tested, not to show our weakness, but to discover our strength."
— *Unknown*

The air was crisp and fresh as I walked home. The sky was that perfect shade of blue that made you feel like you could see forever. The temperature was ideal—not too hot or too cold. I didn't need a sweater, and I didn't sweat as I walked. It was the kind of weather that made you feel good just being outside. In contrast, the city's heat had a way of bringing the sour stench of every garbage can to life, and winter's chill always felt so harsh. But today, the weather felt clean and refreshing.

I had walked this path to and from work for years. Over time, new buildings had gone up, and old ones were torn down or renovated. The neighborhood seemed to be in a constant state of transformation. I could see how the area had evolved into one of those attractive "eat, work, and play" communities while still maintaining the Old Fourth Ward charm.

As I walked, something caught my eye on a billboard advertising a new cell phone. I hadn't noticed the text at the bottom before—it read "Advertising by B&D Media Group." That was the name on the card Mike had given me. It was his advertising group. Why hadn't I seen that before?

Looking up and down the street, I noticed other details I had missed—new streetlights and signs for the coffee shop next to the gas station. I felt like my eyes had just opened after years of sleepwalking. It was as if I was awakening to a new life, filled with gratitude and hope.

When I drew closer to my apartment, I saw a police car parked out front and figured one of my neighbors must be fighting again. Fights were common in the neighborhood—people often clashed because they lacked what they needed, whether it was money, hope, faith, or love for one another.

I climbed the stairs and saw a police officer with Matt in handcuffs. My heart raced, and I could hardly catch my breath. "What's going on? What did he do? Where are you taking my son? Officer, this must be a mistake. Matt, what is going on? What did you do?" I shouted. Matt's eyes flared with anger. "I didn't do anything, Mom. I didn't do it!" he growled. The officer's voice was terse. "Your son is being charged with possessing an illegal substance. He had an ounce of marijuana on him." "Mom, it's not mine. You have to believe me. It's not mine!" Matt pleaded. "Ma'am, we're taking him to the station. You can pick him up after he's been booked. It might take a while, so don't rush." "What station? I don't even know where the police station is!" I exclaimed.

The officer ignored me and put Matt in the police car. They drove off, and I broke down in tears. Why is it that every time I feel like I'm moving forward, it feels like I take two steps back? Who could I call? I couldn't call Ray—he had enough on his plate, and I didn't want to burden him further. I didn't know what else to do. "God, please help me," I prayed as I climbed the stairs. While digging through my pockets for my keys, I found the card Mike had given me. I couldn't call him—I didn't even know him. What if it costs me my job? But the vision had told me there were no coincidences. That thought gave me hope and courage.

I looked at the card and went into the house to dial his number. It was a long shot, but I didn't know what else to do. Mike answered on the second ring. "Mike Bradford." My heart raced. I considered hanging up but took a deep breath instead. "Mike, this is Ruth from the diner." "Hi, Ruth!" he replied cheerfully. "Please don't tell me you're calling to say you changed your mind. I won't accept no for an answer. Whatever it takes, we need you here." "Mike, I don't know how to ask you this, and I understand if you say no, but my son's been arrested, and I have no idea what to do or where to go. Is there any way you can help me?" I asked. There was a brief pause on the line before Mike responded. "Of course I'll help. Where do you live? I'll pick you up, and we'll take care of this right away." I gave him my information and hung up, just as I noticed the other kids standing there, tears in their eyes. Luke was clinging to my waist, crying, "Mommy! Mommy! The police took Matt. Did they take him for good? Is he ever coming home?" Sara's eyes were wide with fear. She looked at me as though she was four again, trying her hardest to stay composed for her younger siblings. "Mommy's going to get Matt. Don't worry, everything will be okay," I reassured them, pulling them into a tight hug. Silent tears streamed down my face as I felt so alone and scared. Then, a flash of memory came from the vision—of me constantly surrounded by God's love and support. I was never truly alone. God was always with me. I had become so disillusioned that I had failed to recognize His presence. I wiped away my tears and took a deep breath. "Look, Matt's going to be fine. We're all going to be fine. A new friend is coming to pick me up, and we're going to get Matt."

I spent the next hour calming and reassuring them. Then, I heard the door buzzer. Only then did I realize that Mike was coming to pick me up at my rat hole of an apartment. I was so embarrassed. I answered the buzzer and, sure enough, heard Mike on the other end. "I'll be right down," I said. "Sara, I don't know how long this will take. Will you be, okay?" "I got this, Mom," Sara said weakly, managing a small smile. I went down the four flights of stairs and opened the door to Mike's smiling face.

"Come on," he said. "Let's go get your son." When I got in Mike's sleek new Mercedes-Benz, I almost forgot what I was about to do. I had never been in a new car before—heck, I didn't ride in cars much at all. In the back seat sat an older gentleman. "Hello," he said. "I'm James McCall, the attorney representing the Bradford family. We'll take care of this in no time, don't worry." Mike got behind the wheel, and we headed to the station. "Tell us what you know about what happened to your son," Mr. McCall asked.

"Well, I don't know much. When I came home, the police were already putting him in the cruiser. Matt said he didn't do anything, and the officer said he had marijuana on him. That's hard to believe. Matt may be distant at times, but he's adamant about not using drugs. He swore he'd never do drugs after my ex died from a fentanyl overdose when his marijuana was laced. Matt was furious and promised he wouldn't touch anything like that. He doesn't even drink. The only thing he cares about is basketball," I explained. Mr. McCall asked how old Matt was, and I told him Matt was only 16. "Any priors?" he asked. I shook my head. "Alright. That simplifies things. I think we have a solid chance of getting him home tonight."

Mr. McCall approached the desk with a "Juvenile" tag when we arrived at the station. He looked like he knew exactly what he was doing. He told the officer he was representing Matthew McInnis, and the officer said he was being processed. Mr. McCall made a call and moved out of earshot. Mike looked at me with deep concern as I started apologizing.

"I'm so sorry I dragged you into this, but I didn't have anyone else to call, and I found your card in my hand," I said. "Hey, it's okay," Mike replied. "Kids get into situations sometimes. It's part of growing up." "Matt is a good kid. I don't know how this could have happened," I said. "He's in good hands. If anyone can handle this, it's James McCall. He's been getting me out of hot water since I was Matt's age," Mike reassured me.

The station was quiet, and we sat in a couple of chairs across from a long counter with bulletproof glass. There was one window with an opening and several desks behind the glass. I didn't see Matt anywhere, just one officer at a desk in the back corner. Mike and I sat in uneasy silence for a few minutes before Mike finally broke it.

"Ruth, can you tell me about yourself? I'm not trying to pry. Whatever you want to share is fine, but if you don't want to, that's okay too. I just want to get to know you better," Mike said. I took a deep breath. "Well, it's a long story." Mike smiled. "I think we have a little time." For some reason, I felt comfortable talking to Mike. Maybe it was his smile. It felt like I had known him my whole life. A sense of peace washed over me, despite all my troubles. I told him how I had gotten pregnant at a young age, how things went with Aaron, and how I had lived day-to-day after my mom kicked me out—staying with whoever would take me in, even spending a day or two on the streets here and there. I shared how I made friends with people who turned out not to be real friends, but for a time, the situation worked. It was tough, but then Ray gave me a job and helped me find an apartment. He became like family to my kids. My life wasn't great, but it wasn't terrible, either. It could've been much worse. I added, "This might sound a little crazy, but despite all the hell I was going through, I always felt like angels were guiding me."

I paused, unsure of how Mike would react. But then, I continued, telling him how I'd searched for love in the wrong places and met Johnny at an outdoor concert in Piedmont Park. We hit it off right away, spending more and more time together. Before long, I found myself living with Johnny. He was good company, with great intentions, and a musician with big dreams, but only finding small gigs that paid next to nothing. We got married and had a decent life until the drugs took him from me. I was left alone to raise four kids with no support.

I couldn't believe I had admitted my belief about the angels. I started feeling foolish for opening up like that when Mike surprised me by reaching over and taking my hand. My heart started racing. My stomach filled with butterflies, and I found myself unable to speak. He looked into my eyes, and it was as if he truly saw me. No one had looked at me like that in a long time.

"I believe in angels too, Ruth. I know we just met, and you don't know me, but I want to get to know you, and I want to help you," Mike said. I let out a small laugh. We both dropped our hands and stood up when we saw Mr. McCall approaching.

"The charges have been dropped," he said. "I looked over the paperwork, and the officer who picked Matt up didn't follow the proper procedures for searching. They had to release him."

Moments later, Matt came through a door, his head hung low, still angry, ashamed, and quiet. We all walked to the car and began the drive home.

"Mike, Mr. McCall, I don't know how to thank you for helping us," I said. Mike smiled in the rearview mirror. "I'm glad I could help." I liked Mike. He was a genuinely good guy, and there was something about him that made me feel a certain way inside. In a soft voice, I asked Matt, "What happened?" Matt recounted the events of his day. He had gone to the basketball court to play after school, as he always did. A few of the guys he usually played with were there. One of the boys had brought his cousin—someone Matt didn't recognize. The kid sat by our bags, watching and smoking a joint. "When the kid saw the patrol car pull up, his eyes widened, and we all turned to see what was going on. The officer went straight to him like they knew each other. 'Okay, buddy, you know the deal,' I heard the officer say. 'Hands behind your head.' Then he started frisking him, and the kid looked nervous for a second, but then he nodded toward us with a devious smile. The officer looked at our bags on the ground and started searching through them. 'I know you have something, buddy. What did you do with it?' he asked. The kid giggled and said, 'I don't know what you're talking about. You searched me, now back off.' That's when the officer picked up my bag and found the marijuana. I got scared, Ma, and told him it wasn't mine. He started coming toward me, and I panicked, so I ran. He chased me, and I could hear him calling it in. By the time I got upstairs, a car was pulling up, and the officer came to the door. The kids were scared, so I opened it. They found me because my address was in the bag. That's when you came home. Mom, the weed wasn't mine. You know I don't do that stuff."

Matt cried and finally broke down. Mr. McCall said, "Son, you don't have to worry about this but let this be a lesson to you. From now on, be more cautious about where you leave your things. That officer didn't like being cited for improper procedure. He'll come back. I strongly advise you to be careful." Matt wiped his eyes. "I'm going to get Buddy for setting me up." "That won't do anything but get you into more trouble. Just drop it," I said. "Buddy will get what's coming to him when the time is right." Mike nodded in agreement as we pulled up to the apartment.

"Thank you!" I said. "I truly appreciate everything you've done. I don't know how I can repay you, Mr. McCall." I elbowed Matt, and he looked up to say thank you too. Mr. McCall smiled. "Don't worry. Mike here has already taken care of the payment. You owe nothing." I looked at Mike, who just shrugged. "He's on retainer, and I want to look out for the company's best interests. You're part of the company now, right?" "Right. I'm part of the B&D Media team. Good night, gentlemen. I'll see you tomorrow, Mike," I said, holding back joyful tears.

Matt and I took the long walk up the stairs. I felt like a ton of bricks had just been lifted off my shoulders. When Matt opened the door, all three kids jumped on him and hugged him. For the first time in as long as I could remember, Matt didn't push them away. Luke asked, "Are you a criminal now? Do you have a record?" "No," Matt said, laughing. Sara smiled. "Matt, I'm glad you're okay." "Me too," he replied.

That night, we stayed close to home and one another. We played Uno, and I made s'mores after dinner. I think each of us was just thankful for what we had escaped.

After the kids went to bed and I finished my regular chores and prepared for the next day, I took a moment to look at the card Mike had given me. Matt was so shell-shocked that he hadn't even asked who Mike and Mr. McCall were. I don't think he cared. All that mattered was that he wasn't going to jail.

I pulled out the sofa bed and lay down, reflecting on what a difference a day can make. Last month felt like a lifetime ago. I said my prayers, thanking God for blessing me with everything that had happened today.

Life is always subject to change without notice. The more rigid we are in our beliefs about what's real, the harder it is to adjust to changes in our reality. I knew that now. My reality had just been shaken to its core, and it would never be the same.

Chapter 13

"Faith is taking the first step even when you can't see the whole staircase."
—*Martin Luther King Jr.*

I woke up the following day feeling conflicted. This past week had been bittersweet. Time had flown by, and now it was Thursday—the last day of work. My heart felt heavy as I thought about the day ahead at the diner, and yet I felt anxious about heading to Mike's office to start the paperwork for my new job. A sliver of sunlight shone through the gap in the curtains, perfectly aligned with a break in the clouds. Was this the hope I needed to hold onto? I asked myself. I lay there, wrestling with my emotions about the changes in my life. I could feel the weight of depression trying to creep into my mind, but I knew I couldn't afford to let it take over. "God, I need you," I said aloud. I got on my knees and began to pray.

"Dear God, maker of all that was, all that is, and all that ever will be, I stand before you, thankful for your greatness, grateful for all the blessings you have just for me, and thankful for whatever is to come. I feel and see it, and I believe that your hand has parted the clouds before me, reaching out to take my hand and guide me to a better place. Lord, help me focus on your light so that it will illuminate my darkest thoughts, revealing them as false illusions of fear. Lord, from 2 Timothy 1:7, 'God has not given us a spirit of fear, but of power, love, and a sound mind.' Thank you, God! Thank you, God! Thank you, God! And so, it is!"

I felt so much better after my prayer. Energized, I sat up to meditate. I closed my eyes and felt the warmth of that lone ray of sunshine relax me. Taking three deep breaths, I began to still my thoughts, focusing on the love of God flowing through me.

As the peaceful feeling of being in God's presence washed over me, I began to visualize new beginnings. I saw myself in new clothes, walking into my office building. I could see myself greeting my coworkers, sitting behind a desk, enjoying my work. I imagined going home to a decent place to live, with my own room. I expressed gratitude for this, or something better, manifesting in my life.

Once I finished, I felt invigorated and grounded. I could hear the children getting ready for school, and I prepared myself for my big day. I thought about this moment in time—a day marking a significant change in my life—and wondered what would stand out in my memories later on. I got up, put away the sofa bed, and went to the kitchen to make coffee and start breakfast. It wasn't long before Sara came in, smiling, and sat down to eat.

"Mom, I want to try out for the cheer team," she said. I looked at her in surprise; she had never shown interest in extracurricular school activities before. "That's great!" I replied. "When are the tryouts?" "They start next week, so I need you to sign this permission slip," she said, pulling a pen and the paper from her book bag. I signed it and said, "You're going to be an excellent cheerleader! I'm so excited for you." I hugged her and kissed her cheek.

As I finished cooking the eggs, Luke and Lydia walked into the kitchen. Or rather, Luke ran in and grabbed me around the waist. "I love you, Mommy," he said. I put their plates on the table, and they all ate. "I love you too, my little superhero," I told Luke. Lydia looked at him and grumbled, "You're not a superhero." "Alright, let's get ready to go to school," I said before they could start arguing. They grabbed their book bags and headed to the door. Each of them gave me a big hug. As they left, I said, "I love you more," and each answered. Luke said, "I love you more than peanut butter and jelly sandwiches." Lydia said, "Bluey." Sara said, "More than watching Disney movies."

Matt, still rattled by the previous night's events, paused longer than expected before saying, "Mom, I love you more than I could have ever imagined. I'm so glad I have you for a mom." He kissed me on the cheek and ran downstairs.

After cleaning the kitchen, I showered and dressed, then hurried to work. The walk to the diner was pleasant, giving me time to appreciate my morning with the kids. In many ways, it felt like just a regular day, but I knew it was a day of change and new beginnings. I had walked this road to the diner for years, and now, with its closing, I would be walking a new path. I took in my surroundings, so familiar they felt like part of me.

As I reached the diner, a wave of nostalgia hit me. Some of the best moments of my life had happened here with these people, and now we were going our separate ways. I had to fight back tears as I opened the door. Ray had the full staff on today, both the day and evening shift. Eileen and Brenda had already started hanging the balloons and putting up the farewell banner. This was really happening. The diner was closing. The new owner was taking it "as is," so Ray didn't need to do anything except clear out the food inventory and lock the doors. It felt almost like a celebration. Ray cooked up everything left in the refrigerator, lowered prices for customers, and offered free meals to the homeless. Every seat in the diner was filled all day, and the take-out line was long. Ray said he was closing at 5 p.m. so we could have a party for the staff. Ray and Eileen were getting ready to travel, and there was a sense of excitement in the air.

A few minutes before my shift started, I went over to Ray. "Ray, I need to talk to you." He waved me into the kitchen while cooking bacon on the grill. "Ray, you remember those guys who were here yesterday?" I asked. "Yeah, you spent the whole afternoon over there goofing off while customers were waiting on you," he replied, chuckling. "I did not!" I said, laughing. "Anyway, they offered me a job and want me to start next week." "Are you serious, Ruth? What kind of job? Are you sure it's legit? I'm not trying to put you down, but you've only worked in the diner. What do they expect you to do?" Ray asked. "It's a receptionist position. Ray, they see something in me that neither you nor I ever saw, so I'm stepping out on faith to see where it leads me." "Never you mind me then. I hope it works out. I know you were getting discouraged about finding a job. If you ever need anything, call me! I'll be here for you as long as I can." Ray pulled me in for one of his big bear hugs. "That's why I needed to talk to you. I need a couple of hours today to fill out paperwork for the new job, if that's okay?" "Of course! Take all the time you need. Eileen can cover. I'm closing early today anyway." "Thanks, Ray," I said. "You know I love you." "Aww, don't get all mushy on me," Ray said, turning his back to me as he fried eggs. "Now get out of here. I hope this works out for you, kid. You're a good mom, Ruth, and you deserve a break."

I looked at some MARTA bus/train schedules Brenda had at the diner to figure out the best way to get to B&D Media's office. It looked like I could take a bus from the corner of my street to a train station and catch the train into Midtown. I'd used this route before, and it felt reassuring that something would be familiar. It only took me 15 minutes to reach B&D Media's office on 10th St. The building was one of Atlanta's tallest and most impressive. The lobby had polished marble floors and glass windows covering almost three stories, a large reception desk with security guards, a few shops, a café, and a seating area.

I asked the security guard at the reception desk how to contact Mike Bradford at B&D Media. He picked up the phone, pressed a button, and then looked at me. "Ruth McInnis," I said quickly. He continued, "Ruth McInnis is waiting for Mr. Bradford in the lobby." He hung up and said someone would come down shortly. I sat near the café, watching the busy people pass through. The lobby was full of deliveries, and people were coming and going. I waited nervously, feeling out of place among the men in business suits and professionally dressed women. I thought about my non-existent wardrobe. How did I expect to fit in here? Then I caught myself mid-thought and knew I had to shift to positive thinking. I imagined myself walking confidently through the lobby, well-dressed and seamless in this vibrant business scene.

After a few minutes, Mike appeared in the lobby. I stood up and started walking toward him. He greeted me with a dazzling smile that made me feel instantly welcome and comforted. I hadn't realized how nervous I was until I saw him.

"Good morning, Ruth! How are you this morning?" he asked as he reached out to shake my hand. "Fine," I replied, feeling somewhat awkward as I shook his hand and smiled nervously. Why did that feel so strange? I had the weirdest sensation inside. It was as if I had known Mike forever and should be hugging him. But this was business, and he was my new boss. He gestured toward the direction he had come from, and we started walking to a bank of elevators. He mentioned that I should always take the elevators on the left because they served the offices on the 14th floor and above. After all, B&D Media's offices were on the 16th floor. We stepped into the elevator, and the doors closed, leaving just the two of us inside. "How's Matt doing this morning?" Mike asked. "Good. I think he's still a little rattled by the whole experience, but I believe it gave him a new perspective on what really matters. I can't thank you enough for being there for us," I said. "I'm glad I could help," he replied. There was a tenderness between us as we momentarily held each other's gaze. The elevator doors opened to reveal a wall made of beautiful dark wood, stretching from floor to ceiling, with the company's name etched in a glass inlay, softly illuminated from behind. Pictures of the company founders, Mr. Bradford and Mr. Dunn, were displayed below.

We turned right upon exiting the elevator and walked through a set of double glass doors leading into the office space that spanned the entire 16th floor. Bold letters in a beautiful script on the glass read, B&D Media Group.

The doors opened into a large area with a half-moon, 12-foot-long receptionist desk—though there was no receptionist present. Mike pointed to the desk and said, "This will be your area." I thought to myself, I really will be the face of first impressions.

We continued down a long hallway and passed through a set of double glass doors with "Human Resources" embossed in frosted letters. HR was a department inside the office. Several individual offices lined the right side, and a conference room sat on the left.

Mike stopped at the last office on the right—a beautiful corner office where a stately, African American woman in her 50s sat behind a desk. She smiled warmly when she saw us. Mike introduced her as Mrs. Annette Harris, the head of HR. "Hello, Ms. McInnis! I've heard so much about you from Mr. Bradford," she said.

Annette wore her hair in a natural style with highlights, and her navy-blue pantsuit paired with a white button-down blouse was stylish yet professional. She stood up, took a folder from a pile on her desk, and walked around to shake my hand. "Let's head to the conference room to get started on your paperwork," she said. We retraced our steps before entering the conference room. Mike nodded toward Annette and said, "Call me when you're done." She sat me down at a conference table with a folder containing my paperwork. She asked me to fill out my application, including my SSN and other personal details. There was also another document labeled "Offer Letter." I looked up in surprise. "Offer letter?" I repeated, smiling. She explained that I could review the letter and make a counteroffer if I wanted to. I'd never received an offer letter before, and I had no idea how or whether I should counter it. Wow. I read the letter over, and my eyes nearly popped out of my head. They wanted to pay me forty thousand dollars a year—more than double what I had been earning at the diner. And they were offering me a two-thousand-dollar sign-on bonus! What in the world was happening? Holy moly, this was unbelievable. I stared at Mrs. Harris, dumbfounded. "Is everything okay?" she asked. "Do you need to change anything?" "No!" I proclaimed. "I'm just having a hard time believing what I'm seeing. This is incredible. Do you really want to pay me this much for doing something I don't know how to do? Why?" "Mr. Bradford obviously sees something in you he really believes we need, something that he believes will help change things for the company. We've been looking for someone to take this position, and he has shot down every applicant." "Most people spend days, weeks, even months searching for a job, and he just walked in and offered me one. I'm a little overwhelmed." I said, "The offer is more than fine."

"Great. Take your time filling out the forms, and I'll be back in a minute to check on you, Ms. McInnis," she said.

It took me about fifteen minutes to complete all the paperwork. I had just put my pen down when Mrs. Harris returned. She picked up my forms and scanned them. "Do you have any questions?" she asked. "Not at the moment," I replied. "If you have any questions later, you can always find me here to provide any additional information you might need next week. Mr. Bradford said you could start on Monday. Is that still the case?" "Yes," I replied. "We'll do a background check and a drug test next week. You'll be on probation for the first sixty days, after which you'll be considered a permanent employee. A temporary badge will get you in the elevator and up to this floor. Your permanent one will come after your probation period and will have your picture on it. Do you need your parking validated today?" she asked. "No, I don't have a car," I replied. "Okay, be here Monday at 8 a.m. You'll receive your sign-on bonus as part of your first paycheck at the end of your third week. We pay bimonthly." I started to worry about how I'd make it to work with so little money over the next two weeks, and I guess Annette could tell by the look on my face. "What's the matter?" she asked. "I didn't realize it would be so long before I get a paycheck," I said. "Unfortunately, that's pretty standard," she said. She called Mike, and a few minutes later, he came back in, beaming. He escorted me back to the lobby and asked if everything was okay. "Yes, more than okay! I'm so happy you offered me this job! Thank you! I'm looking forward to starting Monday morning," I said, grinning.

Several people were on the elevator ride to the lobby, and everyone was silent. We exited the elevator with the others and paused for a moment as we reached the lobby entrance. I turned to him to say goodbye and felt like he would kiss me. What was more surprising was that I wanted him to kiss me. I hadn't felt this way in a long time, and it was more than a little unsettling. "I'm so glad you agreed to join the team. I think you're exactly what we need. I'll see you Monday," Mike said, his voice soft. "Thank you. 'Thank you' doesn't even begin to express my gratitude for this opportunity. Have a great weekend, Mike. I'll see you Monday," I replied. We held each other's gaze for a second longer than necessary.

As I turned to walk away, I heard a woman behind me say, "Hey, handsome, if you're all done with your little admin duties, do you want to get some lunch?" Mike replied, "Sure, Kali, just let me go back up to the office and get my jacket. I've been meaning to call you."

I didn't want to turn and look, but I couldn't help wondering if she was someone special to Mike. I couldn't believe I was jealous of a woman I didn't know. I thought it was ridiculous to feel this way about a man I barely knew, but I couldn't shake it. I continued my journey back to the diner.

I was done with everything by 10:30 and on my way back to the diner. I thought about my tattered and worn wardrobe as I rode the bus back. I didn't have anything to wear, and I didn't have enough money to get through the next three weeks.

The good thing about working at the diner was I would get tips every day and a paycheck every week. But I couldn't see how I could buy work clothes, feed my family, and pay for Marta with the money I had for the next three weeks.

I couldn't let that get me down and send me into negative thinking. Look at all the fantastic things that had happened to me so far. I just had to have faith. God would make a way out of no way. All that was required of me was to believe it!

Chapter 14

"being confident of this very thing, that He who has begun a good work in you will complete it until the day of Jesus Christ;"
—Philippians 1:6

I returned to the diner by noon, and we took orders until 4 p.m. We worked until five on the dot, when Ray shut the diner down. He gave all the remaining customers to-go containers and prepared them to leave. The party was in full swing once the door closed behind the last customer. Ray had invited some of our neighboring business owners, like Johnny from the garage, and previous staff members to help us celebrate. We celebrated Ray and all our new beginnings. Somehow, everyone had managed to find a new job. We danced to the jukebox music, sang, and laughed until Ray called it a day. He allowed each of us to fill a few bags with food from the kitchen. I left with three bags of frozen meat and vegetables. Most importantly, Ray gave me the rest of the cake. Ray forbade anyone from crying. He said, "It's a celebration, and we're all going to leave with a smile." Eileen gave me a ride home, and we said our goodbyes.

The kids were so excited when they saw me walk in with a cake. You would've thought it was their birthday. They rarely had store-bought cake, so this was indeed a special treat. I told them about my new job, which gave them even more reason to celebrate. Matt asked if the job was with Mr. Bradford, who helped get him out of jail. I told the kids about meeting Mike and his friends at the diner, his office downtown, and my new position as "Director of First Impressions." They laughed riotously. Luke's eyes widened with awe: "You're going to be the director!" I giggled and explained that what I would actually be

doing was answering phones. They thought that was even fun-
nier, and we all laughed, having the best carefree evening in a
long time. After dinner and the regular chores were done, the
kids went to bed. I was still working out in my head how I was
going to manage the next few weeks. At least, thanks to the food
from the diner, we wouldn't be hungry.

The next day was my first day off on a weekday in years.
The kids and I went through our usual morning rituals, and then,
I was alone with my thoughts. I decided to do a good house
cleaning and see if there was anything we no longer needed.
Since I was already going to the Goodwill Thrift store, I could
drop off the items before I bought something for myself. I remembered the vision that whatever you give comes back to you,
blessed and multiplied. We didn't have much to begin with, but
after cleaning Matt and Luke's room, I found some clothes that
no longer fit either. The age difference made handing clothes
from Matt to Luke impractical. I knew I had to be very mindful
of my pennies. I had $75 in my pocket for the next three weeks.
I bought a Marta card for $25, which would get me to work for
a week. I would have to walk the few miles home every day. I
had enough food for two weeks now, leaving me with $20 to
find something to wear to work and $30 for lunch.

My trip to Goodwill was a big success. For $20, I found a
couple of lovely skirts and blouses that I could mix and match
with some of the blouses in my closet for a week's worth of outfits.

I got up extra early Monday morning, at least a couple of
hours before the children. I didn't want to be late for my first
day. After my morning prayer and meditation, I took a little more
time in my gratitude journal. I was so moved by the sheer mag-
nitude of the changes in my life, so elated by the opportunities

that lay before me, so awe-inspired by the blessings in my life that I had to write about it. I knew beyond a shadow of a doubt that if Ray had closed the diner before I met Christian, I would have been devastated and fallen into a pit of despair. I wouldn't have been happy and excited when I served Mike's table. I would've been too busy with my pity party to be available for my opportunity.

I remembered parts of the vision that clearly showed me getting in my way by not being present and focusing on the worst possible outcome. Being present, being positive, and being my best brought more goodness into my life. It also brought Mike. I was almost afraid thinking about him. He was so handsome with his chiseled jawline and thick black hair that was kept short and neat. He was about 6'3" and very fit, yet not too muscular. On top of it all, he smelled great. He could be married for all I knew, but he didn't wear a wedding ring. He's my boss and thinking about having more than a work relationship with him could lead to disappointment and heartache, but I couldn't help myself. I haven't been able to stop thinking about him since I first laid eyes on him. I felt our connection, and I believe he felt it too. He is fantastic, and if I were thinking the way I used to about myself, I would've been looking at myself as not good enough—but not anymore. I am awesome. I am amazing. And I am more than enough for Mike. I had to say it a few more times out loud for it to sink in. If nothing more than a great friendship had happened between Mike and me, it would have had nothing to do with me not being good enough. But for the first time in a long time, I wanted more. I looked at myself in the mirror as I applied light makeup, lipstick, and eyeliner. "Ruth, you are beautiful, and I love you!" I said to my reflection and giggled like the schoolgirl I once was. I said it, and I believed it. I knew that I couldn't give love to someone else if I couldn't love myself first.

I cleaned up, and as I dressed in my new clothes, I caught a glimpse of myself in the mirror and thought about how different I looked, even to myself, compared to the lady I glimpsed in the window of the diner not so long ago. It seemed like years ago, but it was only a couple of months. Christian had come into my life and provided a glimpse that changed everything.

Chapter 15

The only thing sweeter than union is reunion.
—Kathleen McGowan

I nervously opened the double glass doors leading to the office that occupied the entire 16th floor of the building. In big, bold letters, the words B&D Media Group were elegantly scripted across the glass. I now work for B&D Media Group. A month ago, I didn't even know who they were—yet here I was. I was thrilled.

Walking through the doors to the receptionist's desk, I found a petite young woman with bright red hair and fair skin. She appeared to be in her early twenties. I smiled and gave her my name. She beamed and extended her hand. "Hi! I'm Kelly, and I'm so glad you're finally here. The secretary pool has been taking turns being the receptionist until they could fill the position. Have a seat, and I'll give Mr. Bradford a call. He was just here looking for you."

I sat down, nervously flipping through a few magazines. The entire place radiated elegance and professionalism. I glanced around at the ads displayed on the walls, surprised to recognize several of them. It was hard to believe that all of them had originated right here, in the office where I now worked. Thankfully, it wasn't long before Mike came around the corner, Jack following closely behind. Both men wore huge smiles, instantly washing away my nervousness. Mike and Jack shook my hand warmly. "Follow me, and I'll show you around," Mike said. We walked down a long aisle with cubicles on the left and offices on the right. Each office had floor-to-ceiling windows offering stunning views of Atlanta. Every name was displayed neatly on a plaque beside each door or cubicle. Most office doors were open, and whenever someone was present, Mike introduced me. I felt like a movie star. Everyone was so kind and welcoming. Mike showed me the three state-of-the-art conference rooms, then led me to the kitchen, equipped with two industrial-sized refrigerators, coffee makers, and microwaves.

One entire wall of the lunchroom featured floor-to-ceiling windows with an incredible view stretching all the way to Stone Mountain. It was breathtaking. I almost expected someone to shake me awake and say, "Okay, Ruth, get back to the diner."

Returning to the reception area, Kelly stood up from behind the massive desk. "All yours," she said warmly. "I'll give you a few minutes to get set up with IT and to get comfortable. Then I'll come back and show you some basics. This binder has almost everything you'll need, including a phone directory and instructions for transferring calls. IT will bring your computer and help you set it up shortly." I sat down and realized—for the first time—I had a job that didn't require me to be on my feet for ten hours a day. Mike and Jack were still smiling from ear to ear. "Please call me if you need anything," Mike said. "I'm so glad you're here," Jack added, giving my shoulder a friendly pat before they both walked away. Spinning around in my chair, I couldn't help but let out a mental shout of joy.

A few minutes later, a man who looked oddly familiar came around the corner. I blinked several times, making sure I wasn't imagining things. It was Aaron. Matt's father. He looked just as stunned as I felt. I hadn't heard from him since he graduated from high school. Aaron put down the laptop he was carrying and pulled me into a hug. "Ruth," he said, "what are you doing here?" I was flooded with emotion. He didn't even know he had a son. Matt looked just like him—those same bright blue eyes and soft, blond hair. My heart ached as I remembered how devastated I was when Aaron left. Losing him hurt even more than my mother throwing me out of the house. Aaron stepped back, holding me at arm's length. "You look great! I haven't seen you since graduation. How have you been?" I wanted to say, "My life has been a mess." I wanted to yell at him for choosing baseball over me. I wanted him to know how deeply he had hurt me. But instead, I smiled and said, "I'm great! I just started my new job here. How about you? I thought you'd still be in California." "Um, no. I'm the IT Manager here. I'm actually here to set up your system," he said with a big grin.

"Wow, this is mind-blowing. I always wondered what you ended up doing after high school. You were so smart—I wouldn't have been surprised if you went on to do something amazing." Standing there, I felt embarrassed—like a failure. Then I noticed the wedding ring on his finger. "I see you're married," I said, trying to keep my voice light. "Yes, almost five years now. We had our first baby last year." "Do you have any pictures?" I asked. "Of course!" he said, pulling out his wallet and showing me a picture of a beautiful baby boy who, at that age, looked like Matt's twin. "Wow, he's adorable. He looks just like his daddy," I said, smiling. Aaron chuckled. "Everyone says that." Inside, I burned with anger. He had the life I once dreamed of—a marriage, a family—and I had nothing but memories and struggle. "How about you, Ruth? Are you married? Any kids?" Aaron asked. I hesitated, tempted to lie, but couldn't bring myself to. "No, I'm not married, but I have four children." "Wow! I can barely manage with one. How do you manage four?" he said, although something in his voice didn't sound completely sincere. "Do you have any pictures of your kids?" "No, I don't," I said quietly. I didn't want to admit that I could never afford professional photos. The only pictures I had were the free ones from school or gifts from kind friends. "Well, you're all set up now," Aaron said. "Just create a password here, and we'll be done." I typed in my password. Aaron stood up, preparing to leave. Inside, I was screaming: How do I tell him about Matt? How do I say I had your baby after all these years? It wasn't something I could just blurt out. "Maybe we can catch up over lunch sometime," Aaron said. "I'd stay and chat, but I have a conference call in five minutes." "That sounds great," I replied, forcing a smile. "Thank you, Aaron."

As Aaron walked away, my heart pounded in my chest, and I felt lightheaded. How in the world was I going to do this? How could I work with Aaron without telling him about his son? I didn't have a choice anymore. This wasn't some random coincidence; it was time for him to know the truth. Taking a few deep breaths, I calmed my heart and regained my composure. I focused on setting up the computer's home screen, arranging the icons I needed to do my job well. For a moment, I just sat there, feeling strange. How could this be? Aaron, working at my new job? It shook me to realize how much anger I was still holding inside. I wanted to hit him upside the head—and at the same time, I wanted to hold him, to touch him. But he was married now. That part of our relationship would never happen again. Still, I shared something with this man he didn't even know about. Guilt crept in. I should have told him when I found out I was pregnant. Matt was his son too. Aaron had a right to know then—and he still had a right to know now. But the bigger question loomed: What was I supposed to do with all this anger and resentment? I thought I had forgiven myself long ago, but clearly, I hadn't. The feelings overwhelmed me, and my thoughts paralyzed me with fear. Would I even be able to work in the same building with him and pretend everything was, okay? Just as I was about to get up and get a glass of water, a flash of my dream returned. I heard Christian's voice in my mind: "Unforgiveness blocks the door from which all blessings flow." Forgiveness was critical—it was the only way to release the negative energy surrounding me. I remembered how dark everything had been whenever I thought about my mother. I once believed I could never forgive her for turning her back on Matt and me. Just days after she threw me out, she packed up her belongings and moved in with some truck driver—without even saying goodbye. No hug. Nothing. She deserted me. In my vision, when I thought about her, the air around me turned dark. My anger and unforgiveness blocked out every ray of hope, creating a growing darkness that pulled at me like a monster tornado, ready to destroy everything in its path. But in the dream, I knew: if I forgave her, the darkness would lift, and the storm would lose its power. I thought about those old feelings—and how I had eventually resolved them. Now, I realized: I had to find a way to forgive Aaron if I ever wanted peace in my life. I had to find a new way to think about this situation—to find the good hidden somewhere within it. After all, Aaron had been just a teenage boy, doing what teenage boys do. Why was I still carrying this anger after all these years?

I placed my hands over my heart and whispered softly, so only I could hear: "I forgive you, Aaron. I also forgive myself. We were both just children. I don't expect anything from you." As the words left my lips, I felt the weight slowly lifting off my shoulders. I knew it wouldn't vanish all at once, but I sent as much love and light as I could into those worn-out pictures of what might have been, allowing them to slowly dissolve into dust within my mind.

****

Christian stood behind her, lifting the weight of unfor-
giveness from her shoulders as she symbolically let it go. He
placed his hands gently on both sides of her head, helping her
shift from her mind into her heart. He sent flashes of the lessons
he had taught her about forgiveness throughout her journey. And
he instilled in her an unwavering truth: the truth will set you free.
Christian knew it wouldn't be easy for her to tell Aaron—So he
readied himself to give her the gentle push she would need.

Chapter 16

"Some souls just understand each other upon meeting."
— *N.R. Hart*

Kelly returned a few minutes later, showed me how the phone system operated, and pointed out the files I might need in the desk drawer. We worked steadily until lunchtime, when another woman approached the desk. Kelly introduced her as Margaret. "Margaret or someone else will always come to relieve you for lunch," Kelly said. "Great! I guess I'll go get something to eat," I said, checking my wristwatch. "How much time do I have?" "You get an hour," Kelly replied.

I decided to look for Mike and thank him again. His office was tucked into the far corner of the building—a large, plush space with a conference table and several chairs. He looked up and gave me a big smile—Mike's million-dollar smile—that completely melted me. "Have a seat," he said. "How's it going so far?" "Fine. Kelly's been showing me the ropes." "We have orientation tomorrow morning for all the new hires who started this month. Take this package with you; it'll give you a chance to read ahead and be prepared to ask any questions. It'll take a couple of hours, so don't worry about what you know or don't know—we'll make sure you have everything you need." I told him I was speechless and didn't know what to say. "Any questions?" Mike asked.

Before I could answer, a voice interrupted, "Darling, are you ready to go to lunch yet? I don't have long—I've got a meeting with your favorite client this afternoon." It was the same woman I had seen talking to Mike in the lobby. She entered the office with a teasing gleam in her eye, but when she noticed me, her expression changed. She was dressed in a beautifully tailored red suit and wore four-inch heels with red bottoms. Her jet-black hair was pulled back into a flawless bun. Ruby red lipstick and matching nail polish completed her look. Her smile shifted into something devious as she turned to Mike and said, "I thought you were all mine for lunch. You're not going to ask me to share, are you, Mike?" Mike looked at her, his expression losing the warmth it had held for me, though he maintained a polite smile. "I wouldn't dream of asking you to share, Kali," he said. Turning back to me, he asked again, "Any more questions?" I stood up and shook my head. "No, I think I'm good for now," I said, quickly walking out of the office, feeling awkward after Kali's interruption. I had wanted so badly to ask him questions about Aaron but couldn't bring myself to say anything.

Lost in thought, I almost ran straight into Jack, who was standing just outside Mike's office. "Looks like my day just got better now that I see you," Jack said with a warm smile. I wanted to hug him. He was the kind of man you wish you had as a father—warm, caring, someone you could tell anything without fear of judgment or condemnation. "You look like you're stuck in the middle of a forest and don't know which way to go. Maybe I can be of some assistance?" he offered. "No, I'm fine, Jack," I said, holding up the orientation packet Mike had given me. "Mike just handed me my get-to-know-the-company package. Looks like it'll take me all day to get through this." "You think so?" Jack chuckled. "Well, let's take a little shortcut. Come into my office, and I'll give you the Reader's Digest version of this great institution. Then we can get down to the important business of getting to know each other. How about it, Ruth?" How could I say no to this big teddy bear of a man? He reminded me of John Walton from The Waltons. "Sure, Jack. That sounds great." "Have you had lunch yet?" he asked. "No, I was just about to grab something and head to the lunchroom." "Why don't you let me take you out to lunch? We can walk down the street to the sandwich shop and chat along the way."

We stopped by his office, about midway down the hall, so he could grab his jacket. His desk was lined with family photos—beach vacations, snowy holidays, and one I particularly loved: a picture of him holding what looked like his newborn grand-daughter asleep on his chest. The photos reflected the warmth of the man standing before me. For the first time in years, I felt comfortable and safe around someone outside of my family at the diner. It was an amazing feeling—to trust someone I barely knew.

As we walked, Jack told me the history of the company and about Mike and his family. They were incredibly successful and affluent, though you wouldn't guess it by looking at Mike. He was a good man—humble, not snobby or entitled like some rich kids. Jack explained it was because Mike's father had done it right. He made Mike work his way up the ladder without special treatment. "Old man Bradford made Mike earn everything. His philosophy was that Mike would appreciate success more and understand what others went through. It worked. Mike couldn't even touch his trust fund until he accomplished three things: graduate college, get a job on his own merit, and lead a successful advertising campaign. Only after that was the trust unlocked." Jack smiled, shaking his head. "Mike could've been resentful like his brother, but he wasn't. He welcomed the challenge and saw it as an opportunity to achieve something truly." Jack's face dark-ened slightly. "Simon, Mike's brother, is a different story. He was diagnosed as being Autistic when he was in his early twenties. Mr. Bradford wouldn't accept the diagnosis and continued to believe that nothing was wrong with Simon. Simon never excelled in school, but Mr. Bradford insisted that Simon go to college. In turn, Simon attended college and graduated, but refused to pay off his student loans. Mr. Bradford gave him a job here, and Simon messed it up so badly that we had to fire him. Mr. Bradford tried to help him, but it was no use. Mike thought his father was too hard on Simon. Simon disappeared into the streets after he lost his job. It took Mike a long time to find him. Simon only gets by now because of Mike's generosity. Mike pays for his apartment and gives him enough to live on. But Simon hates Mike for it—hates him for being a success."

Jack paused. "Actually, that's why we were in your diner the day we met you. Mike hadn't been able to reach Simon, and someone said he stopped by your diner regularly. You probably know him." "Does he look like Mike?" I asked, already sure I would have remembered seeing someone who looked that good in the diner. "No, just the opposite. He doesn't take care of himself at all. He's an alcoholic—and looks it. As a matter of fact, he always wears this old army coat in the winter, patched and worn." A light came on in my head as it dawned on me, he was talking about the guy we all called "Slimy" Simon. He always looked greasy and nasty, like if you touched him, bugs would crawl right up your arm and infest your whole body. "I know who you're talking about. He used to come to the diner every day. You missed him that day because he came in a little later than usual."

"Just as well. No one can help Simon because he doesn't want to help himself. Mike's father passed away last year, leaving B&D to him. Still, he walks around here like he's just another employee. He lives with his mother too—more to keep her company than anything else. She's perfectly independent and still active in all her social circles. You'd love her; she's one awesome lady. But how about you, young lady? Why hasn't some lucky fella grabbed you up and married you?"

"Jack, I have four kids. As soon as a guy hears that, he's off and running. I can't even get a date. It took me a long time to learn that sex isn't love, and just because a guy wanted to have sex with me didn't mean he cared about me. I finally decided to just be a mother and stop looking for Mister Perfect. He doesn't exist for me." "Don't give up just yet. You're still young." "Jack, I'm not a spring chicken. Most guys my age are married, and the ones who aren't don't want to get married. Look at Mike—he's about my age. Is he married?" Jack's eyes glossed over for just a second before he blinked.

"Mike was married," he said. "Married and expecting a baby when his wife was killed in a car accident five years ago. He hasn't dated anyone seriously since. He still goes out and social-izes, but he says he hasn't met anyone special enough to spend that kind of time getting to know." "That's too bad," I said. "Yes, it is. But when the time is right, I believe he will love again," Jack said. We both fell silent for a moment before Jack continued.

"Okay, back to you, little lady. You're not getting off the hook that easily. Tell me about your family." "Well, Jack, it's not a pretty picture," I said. I told him about how my mother became pregnant with me during her first year of college, and how my father died in a car accident before he even knew I existed. I shared the whole sorry story of my life and my kids. At one point, I paused and said, "Now why am I telling you all of this?" Jack laughed and said, "Because I asked—and you needed to tell your story. You needed to hear it out loud to realize what you're finally coming to terms with: you are not a victim of your circumstances. You could be if you wanted to, but you have cho-sen not to be. You have chosen to be the victor.

"Accepting the position at B&D means you've already made that choice in your heart and mind. The world will no longer treat you like a victim—it will admire you for being victorious over the challenges you've faced, and those yet to come. I'm proud of you." The lunch hour passed quickly, and we made our way back to the office. "Thank you, young lady, for joining me for lunch. I hope it's the first of many." "I hope so too, Jack. Thank you!" I said, as I sat back at my desk and watched him walk away. I smiled as Jack's words resonated in my soul. I'm a victor. Hmm. That sounded pretty good. I accepted it.

For the first time, I felt truly comfortable at my desk, like I belonged. I loved watching people walk by; everyone was so friendly. People would randomly stop to chat for a few minutes. At first, I thought they were trying to get to know me, but then it occurred to me that the receptionist was almost like the office bartender—neutral ground. A place you could go to chat and take a break from it all. Mike stopped by every time he entered or left the building—except when he was with Kali. Then, he would simply wave. He was always so busy with meetings and clients.

Chapter 17

The hardest memories are pieces of what might have been.
—Deborah Smith

On my second day of work, Jack insisted once again on treating me to lunch. We went to one of the cafeteria-style restaurants in the building. The salad bar was incredible—unlike anything I had ever seen. I felt like a kid in a candy shop, trying to fit a little bit of everything onto my plate. I didn't like wasting food, so I was careful not to take more than I could eat. Once, when Ray had let me prepare the salad plates for the day, they had sold out almost immediately. Customers said they were so beautiful they barely wanted to eat them. Ray was so impressed that he added salads to the permanent menu. As I assembled my salad at the bar, I glanced over and spotted Aaron having lunch with his wife and baby. They made such a nice-looking couple, and the baby was adorable. It took everything in me not to rush over, scoop him up, and kiss his chubby little cheeks. I was amazed at how much the baby resembled Matt—and how much Matt looked like Aaron.

In that moment, I knew I would have to tell Aaron the truth eventually. I just didn't know how. I didn't know if he would be happy or angry. It almost felt like someone was playing a cruel joke, bringing everything full circle to the very point where my life had once gone off track. Sometimes life gives you a rare opportunity—to make a different choice than you did before—and maybe this was mine.

I sat down with my back to Aaron. Jack noticed something was off and asked if everything was okay. Before I knew it, the whole story about Aaron and Matt spilled out. I told Jack that I knew I had to tell Aaron and that I would—as soon as I could summon the courage. Jack patted my hand and said, "You know, this isn't just some random accident that you two are working in the same place. This is an opportunity—one to make things right. From what you've told me about your son, a father is exactly what he needs right now. I've known Aaron for a few years, and he's a great guy. No way he would turn his back on his son. He is a basketball coach for an inner-city team and has been a huge influence on several wayward young men. Why don't you let me introduce you to his wife?" I wasn't ready to meet his wife yet. I doubted I could even arrange my face to look innocent, rather than like the guilty cat who swallowed the canary. "Not just yet, Jack. Maybe next time we see them," I said. "I understand. It's a lot to handle all at once. We'll get through this together. Now, tell me more about your kids so I can start bragging about my new grandkids," Jack chuckled. My heart swelled with love for this man. He was the father I had always wanted—and now he wanted to claim my kids, too. It felt like he was stepping up to fill the enormous void that losing Ray would leave in my life.

The rest of the day passed uneventfully. At five o'clock, people started gathering their things and heading home. Mike stopped by on his way out and said, "Alright, that's enough for today. We don't believe in working late or overtime without a good reason. Family's important, and you've got one waiting for you tonight. I'll see you in the morning." He waved and headed toward the elevator, with Kali running after him, asking him to hold the doors.

Well, you don't have to tell me twice—I'm out of here. I grabbed my purse. It was such a nice feeling to leave work and still have energy left. I thought about wandering around downtown, window shopping and savoring life a little, but I knew the kids would be bubbling over with excitement, eager to tell me all about their day. So, I made an executive decision: I ran to the corner just in time to catch my bus home.

Chapter 18

But when he saw the wind, he was afraid and, beginning to sink, cried out,
"Lord, save me!" Immediately Jesus reached out his hand and caught him.
"You of little faith," he said, "why did you doubt?"
—Matthew 14:30-31

I managed to maintain my routine of praying, meditating, and doing visualizations every morning before work. I wrote in my journal every night. Although I was clearly on my path to true bliss, I knew there was still much more ahead. The path wasn't smooth sailing—it was filled with potholes, setbacks, sacrifices, and challenges. It became clear that true bliss wasn't about possessions, money, or material wealth. It was about the internal wealth I was building inside myself, now beginning to manifest in my physical world. None of this would have been possible without love and intention. I had to be deliberate in my efforts to be grateful, to forgive, and to give of myself. I had to dig deeper, believe it was possible, and step out on faith to receive it!

****

Christian stood beside her as she practiced using her spiritual tools. He brought clarity to her realizations and energized the depth of her visualizations. These moments were pivotal for her, anchoring her in the understanding that she was in the presence of, and connected to, something greater than herself.

****

The rest of the week was packed with new information, getting up to speed with the ever-evolving world of technology. B&D felt like I had finally found a new home. Jack and I shared our little chats every day. I learned that Jack was from New England, married with two sons and two granddaughters. He also had one brother, Maurice, who was married with two daughters and a grandson. Jack's parents had both passed away, and he was very close to his brother. He told me how growing up, they used to fight constantly, but after Maurice nearly died in a car accident, their bond grew much stronger. "The threat of death can change your perspective," Jack said. "My brother was in a coma for almost a month. We thought we had lost him. Now, our families vacation together and spend almost every holiday together. I can't wait for you to meet them." I listened with a longing to have a big, loving family of my own. Jack was truly a blessed man.

Mike also stopped by my desk often to chat, and I found myself looking forward to seeing him. There was an undeniable pull toward Mike that I couldn't explain. He wasn't just attractive—he was genuinely kind. I hadn't thought about another man like that since Aaron, but Mike felt completely out of my league. He was my boss and probably already involved with Kali. Still, I couldn't understand why he was paying me so much attention if he was with her.

Saturday morning, the door buzzer rang. I was surprised to hear Ray's voice. Considering his ALS diagnosis, I didn't want him climbing four flights of stairs, so I quickly told him I'd be right down. "Hey, Ray! What are you doing here?" I asked. "I wanted to come by and give you your severance pay," he said. "And I found this notice taped to your front door." He handed me an envelope full of cash and a piece of paper. "It's two weeks' pay, plus what you would have made in tips—a total of $2,000. I wanted to thank you for everything you did to make the diner the success that it was. Looks like you could use it right now."

I looked at the notice. It was an eviction notice. The building was being torn down, and all tenants had 90 days to move out. "Just great," I thought bitterly. While the money would definitely help, I knew it wouldn't be enough. "Don't you worry, Ruth!" Ray said brightly. "It'll all work out. How's that new office job going? I'll bet that helps." "It's good, Ray, really good," I replied weakly, still reeling from the shock of the eviction notice. "I'll be back around Christmas for that trip to Disney World with you and the kids," he added. "Don't tell them! Let's make it a surprise—we'll leave the day after Christmas." He gave me a big hug, walked down the steps, got into his car, and drove away.

As I watched Ray drive off, I noticed a man in a hoodie down the street, watching me. I stared back for a moment before turning away. A heavy feeling sank into my chest. The fear of trying to find a new home gnawed at me. Negative thoughts began taking root, sharp spikes of fear shooting through my body. I couldn't go back to being homeless again. My chest constricted; my breathing grew shallow. I sank down on the steps, tears spilling onto the ground. I had a good job, but it wasn't going to be enough to secure a new apartment. I didn't have enough money. My credit was terrible. Three months wasn't enough time. As I cried, my gaze landed on an ant dragging a crumb twice its size across the sidewalk. The ant never considered that the crumb was too big—it simply grabbed it and kept moving. In a flashback to my vision, I heard Christian's voice: "It's not the size of the problem that defeats you. It's the size of your belief."

Positive thoughts are the building blocks for manifesting your desires. Doubt, fear, and worry will halt all forward progress. Negative thoughts can destroy you—and your dreams—while feeding the darkest corners of your mind. Wiping my face, I took a deep breath and exhaled slowly, imagining all the negativity leaving my body. Staying true to the teachings from my vision was difficult, especially in moments like this. I had to have faith that everything would work out. I had to envision my family in a new home and believe it was already ours. My thoughts and emotions were critical during challenges like this. I had to be thankful for what I had now. I looked down at the money Ray had given me. I was so amazed—and profoundly grateful. This money was right on time. Thank you, God. You are always here when I need You—right on time.

Chapter 19

"There is nothing concealed that will not be revealed, nor secret that will not be known."
-Luke 12:2

Christian knew she had put off doing what she needed to do. He had whispered to her softly and he had touched her dreams, but still, she would not take the next step to clear her path. Her fear was too great. He would have to force the situation.

****

The next couple of weeks went by so quickly. I worked hard to develop relationships with the clients and vendors. The brief little chats with Mike were the highlight of my day, followed by lunch with Jack. We didn't go out to lunch every day because that wasn't in my budget. Jack would often join me in the break room while I enjoyed my lunch from home. Mike was slowly opening up to me about his life, just a morsel of information here and there. Although I felt like we were bonding, I still felt something standing between us. Was it his grief for his late wife, Kali or was it my secret about Matt and Aaron? Had Jack told him?

Still, I felt like I was settling into my new life, and everyone seemed to be adjusting. I finally got my first paycheck with my bonus, and we all went shopping. I promised everyone a new outfit and another outfit from Goodwill. The kids were all smiles. Matt hated shopping with us, and after he picked up his stuff, he asked if he could go to the video arcade until we were ready to go home.

Loaded with several bags, we were all finally ready to go home. We walked to the video arcade to find Matt. Luke was bursting with excitement about the opportunity to play some games. Luke had never been to the arcade before, and I could only imagine his reaction. As we approached the video arcade, I saw Matt talking to a man. It was Aaron. Oh crap! How could this be happening? My mind started reeling. What were they talking about and how did they end up together? Matt saw me and started waving. Luke ran to him and jumped, landing a flying leap at Matt. Aaron's face twisted in a look of surprise.

"This is your son?" Aaron asked. I could see him making mental calculations in his head. His expression changed to a look of indignation. "Yes, I see you have met Matt," I responded. "Yes, we did meet. We started playing a friendly challenge game of basketball here in the arcade. My wife is shopping, and I get bored, so I always come down to the arcade," he said flatly. Seeing the two of them side by side was scary, there was no denying this.

"Well, I better get going, let's talk tomorrow," Aaron said with a look of concern. "Matt, this was fun. Maybe we can do this again sometime soon." Aaron said, patting Matt on the back and turning to walk away. I recognized I was breathing heavily, and I turned to see Matt staring at the reflection in the arcade mirror of him and Aaron standing side by side. "Mom, how do you know him," Matt asked. "He works with me," I said. "Is that all? You act like you know him more than work or something." Matt asked. "I knew him when I was a kid your age. We went to school together." I said a little defensively. "Is that all?" Matt asked. I paused for a minute. Matt asked again, "Is it?" but with more anger in his voice. I couldn't utter another word. "Is what, is what," asked Luke. Matt stormed off.

"Wait, Matt!" I called after him. He kept walking. I should have told him sooner. I should have told him right away. I had always heard that everything done in the dark comes to light.

And now this had come around full force. What would I say to Aaron tomorrow? I was so scared. Would I lose Matt? What would or could Aaron do? I gathered up the kids and left the mall. They were all full of questions. What's wrong with Matt? What was he talking about? Why is he mad? Where is he going? How is Matt going to get home? One question right after another. I steadied my voice and told them, "All of you, just listen. Matt will be fine. He has some things to think about. He'll be home later."

It was late when Matt finally strode through the door. Everyone else was in bed, and I was sitting on the couch praying for guidance. Praying for the right thing to say the right thing to do. He looked at me and just shook his head. His whole body was tense with anger. "Why didn't you tell me?" Matt asked. "Tell you what? That, that man was your father. I didn't know how to tell you, Matt," I said, flustered. "How do you tell your son that you went to work and there was your son's father after seventeen years of not seeing him or knowing anything about him? How do you start that conversation? Hi Matt, guess who I ran into today at work, your dad. He looks great. He's married and has a kid, oh another kid."

"He seems like a great guy. Why didn't he stay in my life? Why did he leave? What did you do?" "Matt, I was young and before I knew I was pregnant, your father broke up with me to concentrate on baseball, He was being recruited and wanted to put all his focus on the game. By the time I became aware I was pregnant, he had graduated and left town. I loved him with all my heart, and I was devastated. When I told your grandmother, she put me out. The only place I could find that would take me in was a shelter on the other side of town for unwed mothers. I left and never looked back. It was different back then. We didn't have computers at our fingertips, if you didn't know a phone number or address, or know someone who did, it was impossible to find him. I didn't know how to reach him. I saw him for the first time since high school, the first day I went to work. I was as shocked as you are now seeing him. I didn't know how to tell either one of you."

"Is that why you asked me those questions a few weeks ago about having a father in my life?" "No, not then. I hadn't started my job when I asked you before. Matt, I wanted to tell you the day I saw him, but I didn't. I thought I would figure out how to tell you. I thought I had time to do this the right way if there is a right way, I said. Look, Matt, I made a huge mistake. Now you are going to have to make some decisions. Are you going to be angry at me or are you going to be able to forgive me and let it go? The anger will never do anything good for you, Matt. Anger will only lead you to make decisions that you will regret. Take some time and think it over. I'll talk to him tomorrow. He may not want to have a relationship with you, it's something you must consider." I said.

"I may not want to have a relationship with him either," Matt said, storming into the room he shared with Luke and slamming the door. I sat there for a while, still praying for guidance. Slowly the door opened, and Luke came out and snuggled up on the couch next to me., "I can't sleep," he said. "There's a monster in my room." "That's no monster, that's just your brother acting like a monster. We all act like a monster every once in a while, and that's okay as long as we realize we are not monsters and we can stop being one anytime we want to," I said. "But when is Matt going to stop being a monster? He's always spitting fire like Godzilla." Luke whispered. "I don't know, baby, I hope it's very soon," I said, pulling him close. "Me too!" Luke said. I picked him up and took him into bed with me. I knew he would never sleep in his bedroom with Matt that angry. Luke was way too sensitive for that.

Chapter 20

"What if, today, we were grateful for everything?"
— *Charlie Brown*

The next day, when I got to work, Aaron was waiting at my desk. Before I could even take my coat off, he said, "That's my son, isn't it?" I looked him straight in the eyes and replied, "Yes, Aaron. He is your son." "Why didn't you tell me?" Aaron asked. "I didn't tell you because I was angry. You had moved on with your life. When I finally realized I had to tell you, I didn't know how to find you. I didn't know where you were or how to reach you," I explained. "Ruthie, you were my first love. I've thought of you often over the years," Aaron said quietly. "How was I supposed to know that?" I cried. "Never in my wildest dreams did I think you had my child. If I had known, I would have found a way to be there for you and Matt. He's an amazing kid. We had such a good time together. We have so much in common—he's just like me. We connected almost instantly. It wasn't until I saw our reflections in the storefront window on the way to the arcade that it occurred to me how much we even look alike. I told my wife I thought he was my son, and she's anxious to meet him if that's okay," Aaron said. "Well, it's not all up to me. Matt has something to say about it too. I'll tell him you want to see him when I get home tonight," I said. "Ruthie, if you don't mind, I'd rather talk to him myself. What time does he get out of school, and where does he go? I'll be there when he gets out, and we'll see if we have a path forward," Aaron said.

"Wow, you want to be in his life? That would be heaven-sent. He needs someone to show him how to be a good man. He looked just like your son does now when he was a baby—

they could have been twins," I chuckled. "I hate knowing now that I missed so much of his life. Honestly, I probably wouldn't have been any good back then anyway. I was self-centered and focused only on baseball. I've been in Atlanta this whole time. I turned down UCLA's offer and went to Georgia Tech on a full baseball scholarship, majoring in Computer Science. I've done a lot of growing up since then, and I can be a much better father now than I could have been then," Aaron said.

I was floored. Aaron had been in Atlanta the entire time. We had been in the same city—me struggling and him living his best life. I was immediately annoyed but pushed it aside. I gave him Matt's school information and the best time to find him. Aaron looked at me, and a slow smile grew across his face. "We have a son," he said softly. Then, more seriously, he added, "I can help support him financially, Ruthie. I want to help." I was speechless. That was the last thing I expected from this conversation. "We can talk more tomorrow after Matt and I spend some time together," Aaron said, puffing out his chest with pride before marching away.

After work, I went home and found Matt smiling. "I played basketball with my father tonight. We talked—a real talk. I like him, Mom. He's going to help me work on my basketball skills. He coaches a team of kids a little younger than me and said he'd love for me to help. I told him I'd like that," he said. "That's nice, Matt. I'm so happy for you and Aaron," I said. "I'm tired, Mom. Meeting my dad was fire and now I'm burnt out. I'm going to bed." He walked into his room and closed the door. "Thank you, God," I whispered with a sigh of relief. This couldn't have turned out any better.

Over the next month, as I learned the ropes at work, Matt grew closer to Aaron and transformed into a different kid. He wasn't as angry. He was far more patient with his siblings and talked about being "the man of the house" and setting a good example. I almost fell out of my chair the first time he took the trash out without being asked! Aaron's influence was powerful, and I was happy they found each other.

At work, I was learning more and more about my responsibilities. Mike had been right—I was good at it. I became the face they needed. Jack often encouraged me by letting me work on projects for Coca-Cola and the Falcons. I offered my insights and ideas, and he actually used some! It thrilled me every time I saw one of my ideas reflected in a billboard ad or a commercial.

During my 60-day review, Mike and Jack told me how impressed they were with my progress. They wanted me to consider working directly on client projects and even offered to pay for any school studies related to the job. I would continue as a receptionist until my six-month review, but if things kept progressing, they'd start looking for a new receptionist and promote me.

Meanwhile, the guy in the hoodie kept showing up. He watched me come and go every day. Some days, I could even sense him following me to the bus stop. Once, I gathered enough courage to walk toward him, but he quickly turned and disappeared into the shadows before I could get close. I could never quite see his face.

Every day, I spent at least an hour talking with Jack. Some conversations were deep and personal; others were just us joking around. I told him everything about Matt and Aaron, and in the way only Jack could, he listened without judgment or disapproval. I hadn't seen much of Kali, which was fine with me. I never felt comfortable around her—always judged, like she thought she was better than me.

One evening, as I got into the elevator to go home, I heard Kelly call, "Hold the door!" I held it, and she entered with Kali. They were deep in conversation about Thanksgiving. Kelly was headed to St. Marys, GA, to visit her family. Kali mentioned that her family and Mike's family had spent Thanksgiving together at her father's estate in Savannah for as long as she could remember. As they got out of the elevator, I caught one last snippet—something about her father and Mike's father graduating from the same Naval Academy class. I mulled over what I heard on the way home.

Mike and Kali had known each other forever and moved in the same circles. How could I ever compete with that?

This Thanksgiving was special. It was the first one where we could afford a full spread. Sara was thrilled—she made a grocery list, a menu, and cooked the best Thanksgiving dinner we had ever had. Jack had gone to Massachusetts with his family, and Mike had taken his mother to visit her sister Joyce in Florida, much to my surprise.

Everyone returned to work on Monday, overstuffed and ready for the holiday season.

Every year, a professional company decorated the office on the Monday after Thanksgiving. The Christmas kickoff came with cookies in the break room and free Panera lunch for everyone. The kids' Christmas party was set for this Saturday, and the company party for the following Saturday. I considered skipping the party—I had no date and nothing to wear—when Mike called me into his office. "You know you have a seat at the VIP table because of the win on the last project with Jack," he said. "I didn't know that," I replied. "I was thinking about not even attending." "You don't want to make that mistake. We give out great prizes at these parties," he said. "Well, I guess I'd better find a new dress," I said, laughing. "Do you have a date?" Mike asked. I tittered. "A date? What's that? I haven't had one since before Luke was born," I said, thinking about the consequence that followed that last date. "Well, how about you come as my date?" he asked. The look of surprise on my face caught him off guard. "What about Kali?" I blurted. "Aren't you going with her?" "Why would I go with Kali?" he asked, amused. "I thought you two were together," I said. Mike looked down and chuckled. "Kali might want that, but I've never seen her as anything more than a friend," he said. "So... will you be my date?" he asked again. "Me?" I said, stunned. "Yes, you. I can pick you up at six, if that's okay?" "Isn't there a policy about dating management?" I asked cautiously.

"Ruth, at this point, I make the policy, and I have never made one like that. All I ask is that people use good judgment when combining their personal and business affairs. If a relationship interferes with someone's work performance, it is treated like any other thing that interferes with their work performance. If they don't fix it after all the warnings, then we have no choice but to let them go. Some folks will hang themselves and others will be fine. It doesn't affect pay or promotion or even the content of the job because the board makes all those decisions, and it is never left to one person. This takes favoritism out of the equation. I set things up that way some time ago to establish the fairest way of doing business and treating my employees. Since we started doing things this way, I haven't had one case of anyone feeling like they have been slighted because of their race, gender, family status, or relationship status. The board makes all the decisions once reviewed. I don't even get to offer my opinion." "Well then, I guess it's a date," I agreed, walking out of Mike's office unable to suppress a smile. Finally, some time with Mike!

Chapter 21

"Winning doesn't always mean being first. Winning means you're doing bet-
ter than you've ever done before."
—*Bonnie Blair*

I had forced myself not to think about Mike in any way other than work, but now everything had changed. He was handsome, kind, and an all-around great guy. I loved being around him. He was funny, charming, and always a gentleman. I couldn't afford to fall in love with him and risk getting hurt again, but I was starting to think it might already be too late. It would be too difficult to work in the same office and on the same projects if things went badly. For now, this would just be a date—one day at a time. Let tomorrow take care of itself.

The kids' Christmas party was first. I had expected it to be geared toward the younger kids, but they had something for everyone. Luke loved it because it was a party. He played games, ate cupcakes, and made friends with every kid there. I saw Lydia giggling with a group of girls her age, while Sara tasted and studied the food as though she were trying to figure out how to make it. They came home with more stuff than they'd accumulated in a lifetime. I had never seen my children so filled with joy. My heart ached to see them enjoying themselves. Mike finally met all my children. He and Luke became fast friends, and I was amazed to see how shy and reserved Lydia had taken to Mike. He gave us a ride home, and it felt so natural for us all to be in the car and have a good time.

Jack invited us to Christmas dinner with his family. He said his wife insisted he bring home his new daughter. His brother and their family were flying in from Massachusetts. We had never spent Christmas with anyone else; we usually spent a quiet day at home. Aaron had asked if Matt could spend part of the day with him and his family. He wanted Matt to meet his grandparents, aunts, and uncle. It felt strange that Matt now had a whole new family to get to know. I felt bad for the other kids, because they wished their father were still alive to show up and be as awesome as Aaron was with Matt.

I would have loved to have my father in my life, but my father was dead. My mother said he died in a car accident before I was born. I knew very little about him, other than his name was Moe, and they met during her first year—her only year—of college in New England. My mother never talked much about my father, and when she did, she wore a strange, almost sad expression. Whenever I asked, she would always change the subject. There was no information on my birth certificate; the line for my father's name was left blank. After a while, I just gave up. She didn't want me to know for some reason, so I accepted it. I couldn't believe I had done the same thing to Matt for so many years. I was glad he was no longer in that cycle and prayed he never had children not living under his roof.

The office Christmas party was fantastic. The company went all out. They had the best buffet I'd ever seen, an open bar, and even a DJ for dancing. Jack was there with his wife, and they shared a table with Mike and me. Jack's wife, Julia, was wonderful, as beautiful as she was kind. She was a beautiful woman, easily in her 60s but could have passed for someone in her 50s. Her long blonde hair, with grey highlights, flowed straight down her back. She wore a beautiful evening dress with black velvet and tiny sequins. We hit it off immediately, becoming fast friends. Mike was the perfect gentleman all night. We even danced. Kali came over to our table and tried to get Mike to dance with her, but he told her his dance card was full for the foreseeable future. I never dreamed I could be in the arms of a man like him. I never thought a man like him would even notice I was alive. Yet here I was, with a man who looked more like the man of my dreams than anyone I'd ever dreamed of. I felt like Cinderella, and I kept thinking the clock would strike midnight, and I'd have to run out before I turned back into a waif. I listened to my thoughts. How self-defeating they were! Why was I belittling myself? I didn't need anyone else to say anything bad about me—I did it enough. I thought back to the vision I'd had so long ago, a vision as clear as yesterday, and remembered how harmful my negative thoughts were. Every evil thought had a corresponding and disabling manifestation in my life unless I overcame it with a more compelling, positive thought. I started thinking I deserved a man who loves, cherishes, and wants to be with me. I started thinking that God had the right man for me, at the right place and the right time. I believed that the right man was Mike, and that the right time was now.

The final event of the night was the raffle. There were three prizes remaining. The first drawing was for a weekend all-inclusive trip for two at the Hotel Bardo in Savannah. The second prize was an iMac computer system, and the last prize was a 60" television. Mike went up to the stage, took the microphone, and said, "Now, for the real reason you all came tonight—the raffle! Everyone, pull out your tickets. I'll pull a ticket from the jar, and the prize goes to the ticket holder with the last three digits: 802! Who has the winning number?" Kelly started screaming, "I won, I won!" She was practically vibrating with joy. She ran up to the stage to get the envelope with her prize, jumping up and down. "Okay," Mike said, "congratulations, Kelly! I know you'll have a great time. Let me go a little deeper for our next ticket. Okay, the second prize ticket ends with 778. Who is the lucky winner?" A young African American guy I'd seen only a handful of times at the office stood up and walked to the stage. "Congratulations, Donovan!" Mike said. Smiling from ear to ear, the young man shook Mike's hand and said, "Thank you!" Mike handed him the box with the computer in it. Digging his hand into the jar again, Mike said, "The last prize of the night goes to ticket 848. Who is our lucky winner?" I looked around for a moment, finally remembering to check my ticket. "I won! I won!" I screamed. "Congratulations, Ruth!" I was so excited. I had never won anything before in my life. The kids would be beside themselves to get a new television.

The party was over, and we were on our way home, still high on life. Mike had me laughing all the way home as he talked about the freaky dances, he'd seen that night and all the other things I'd missed our coworkers doing. I had won a 60-inch HDTV, and I knew the kids would be thrilled. Wanting to hide it until Christmas, Mike kindly offered to bring it over after they went to sleep on Christmas Eve. We were sitting in his car, talking after Mike had pulled up in front of my apartment building. I didn't want the evening to end. I didn't want him to leave, but I also knew I couldn't invite him up to my apartment. He took my hand, and when I met his gaze, the tenderness melted me. I wanted so much more in that moment.

"I like you, Ruth," Mike said. I want to see more of you outside of the office. I want to take you on dates, I want to get to know your kids, and I want to be a part of your life." My heart was beating out of my chest, my mouth went dry, and I was lost for words. "Please tell me you want the same thing, Ruth. If you don't feel the same way, I'll respect that, and we can be friends. However, I truly hope you feel the same way."

I started speaking even before I had a chance to form a coherent sentence. "Yes, yes, sure, I mean, what I am trying to say," I said, giggling to hide my confusion. "I want the same thing. Yes, I want to spend time with you. It's just that it's been a long time for me and the feelings I have for you are a little scary."

"I know what you mean," Mike said understandingly. "I haven't wanted to spend time with anyone since I lost my wife, that is until the day I met you. You turned something on in me, you brought me back to life. It's hard to explain but I can breathe when I'm with you. Life has more meaning when you're in it. I spend every day thinking of ways to be close to you."

He pulled me closer and gently kissed my lips. As he began pulling away, I reached my right hand to his cheek and pulled him in for more. But I also knew if I didn't get out of that car right this minute, I would ask him to take me home with him. I pulled back, brushing my hand across his cheek.

"Good night, Mike," I said as I opened the car door and got out. Mike exited the car and walked with me up the pathway to the door. "Thank you for the best night I've had in years, Ruth! I look forward to more like this." I was grinning from ear to ear until I noticed the hooded guy watching from across the street. Mike saw my expression change, and with concern, he said, "What is it, Ruth?"

"That guy over there is always watching me," I said. But when I looked back up, the guy was gone. "What guy? I don't see anyone." Mike replied. He held me close for a minute. "I'm okay," I said, "maybe it was nothing." Let me see you safely inside before I go. Flick the lights when you are in your apartment," Mike said. My smile returned as I watched him, watching me. 'My knight in shining armor,' I thought to myself.

Chapter 22

"First best is falling in love. Second best is being in love. Least best is fall-ing out of love. But any of it is better than never having been in love."
— *Maya Angelou*

Mike and I grew closer over the next couple of weeks lead-ing up to Christmas. We spent hours talking on the phone in the evenings, discussing everything under the sun. I told him how excited I was for this Christmas. For the first time ever, I would be able to give my kids a real Christmas. Not that we hadn't had great holidays without big gifts—those were always special. But this year, it made me feel so good to have something under the tree that would make their faces light up with joy. I had saved enough money from my paychecks to buy the kids at least one toy they wanted and some clothes. It wasn't much, but it was more than I had ever been able to do before. On top of that, Ray was coming back to take us to Disney World.

I felt the warmth of the Christmas spirit, not that I hadn't felt it before, but this time, it was all the love and positivity in my life brightening up the holiday. In the past, we'd made some-thing for each other and told the recipient what it was and why we made it for them. Some of Luke's creations were too funny for words. Last year, he made Matt a rope with knots in it and told him it was the beginning of a basketball net he could even-tually put on his hoop. Sara had found time to make aprons for the younger kids in Home Economics. They were so creative. Matt drew funny cartoon pictures that had the kids laughing. It wasn't much, but we had each other, and that was all that truly mattered. Mike said he almost envied the simple, non-commer-cial Christmas we shared. He said it felt more genuine.

The office closed for Christmas week until January 2nd, giving me my first real vacation. I could never afford to take time off from the diner, as it was unpaid. Now, I would get a mini-vacation and still be paid. So many people take the little things for granted.

I pulled out my journal and read over the many blessings I had acknowledged each day. Writing in it every morning had made everything seem brighter. I had been writing in my journal every single day since I had the vision, and now it was almost full. I would need to buy a new one soon.

It was Christmas Eve, and all the kids had finally gone to sleep—even Luke, who had tried to stay awake to see Santa. I called Mike, and he said he was on his way. I did what I could to help him get the TV out of the car and into the apartment. We struggled up the four flights of stairs, collapsing with exhaustion when we finally set the box down. "I don't know if I was much help," I said. He took the TV from the box and set it on the stand. He had wrapped a big red bow around it. "It's beautiful, Mike. The kids are going to scream."

After that, Mike went back to his car to get a bottle of wine and asked if I would like a glass. "Sure," I said, "why not?" I grabbed two glasses. As Mike uncorked the bottle, he looked at me seriously, and I wasn't sure what it meant. Pouring the wine, he said, "Ruth, what do you want in this life? What does your heart yearn for? What do you see yourself having, doing, and being in your dreams?" That was a good question, one I had answered in my journal every day for months. But how could I put it into words I could share? "I don't know how to explain it," I replied. "Don't think with your head, think with your heart. What does your heart long for? What excites you when you think about doing it? What would you do for free if money wasn't an issue? That's the question I want you to ask yourself," he said. I hesitated at first. I wanted to share with him the vision I had when I met Christian, but I was afraid he might think I was crazy. Then again, if this man was going to be part of my life, I needed to know how he would react now, not later. "Mike," I said, "I want to share something with you that might sound a little odd. I hope you can listen with an open heart and mind." "I'll always have that for you," Mike said.

So, I told him the whole story, from the day I met Christian to everything that had happened up until this Christmas Eve. I told him I knew what I wanted and had written about it daily. I was doing exactly what I had dreamed of doing at his company. He listened with fascination and growing interest. We talked nearly until dawn when I finally noticed the time. I told him he should go— the kids would be up as soon as the sunlight hit. He stood up and looked at me in a way I had never seen before.

"Ruth," he said, "I haven't felt this way about anyone in a long time. I think we have something special, and taking a page from your journal, I'm going to tell you that I'm incredibly grateful that you came into my life." He took me in his arms and kissed me tenderly. "Merry Christmas, Ruth," Mike said as he pulled away and handed me a small, beautifully wrapped jewelry box. "Oh, Mike!" I exclaimed. "I didn't get you anything." "You've given me the greatest gift of all, Ruth," he said softly. "You've given me love." I opened the box and found a beautiful bracelet with several charms. "It's beautiful!" I cried. It was the first present anyone, other than my family, had given me in years. "Thank you!" He kissed my cheek and said, "HO! HO! HO! Merry Christmas, Ruth," as he walked out the door. "I'll see you tomorrow at Jack's."

Chapter 23

"True belonging doesn't require you to change who you are; it requires you to be who you are."
— Brené Brown

The next morning, after managing to get only two hours of sleep, the kids woke up and began jumping on my bed, yelling about the new TV. They screamed, bounced, and screamed some more. Luke started crying, "Mommy, Santa bought us a TV! Mommy, Santa bought us a TV!!!!"

"Wow, he sure did," I said, pretending to be surprised as I lifted my head from the pillow. Matt finally came out of his room to see what all the noise was about, and the smile on his face made it all worth it. He looked at the TV, then at me. "How did you manage that?" he asked. I whispered that I had won it at the office Christmas party.

The kids opened their toys and played while I went back to bed for a couple more hours. The question Mike had asked me kept swirling in my mind, and I couldn't stop thinking about it. I wanted him. That much, I knew for sure. I wanted a life with him. I wanted to grow old with him.

I remembered from the vision that when you write something down and see it every day, it helps bring what you truly desire to fruition. So, I took some cardboard from the TV box and drew pictures of what I wanted: a home, a car, a picture of a man and a woman together. I drew my kids, happy and healthy, and a big family gathering. When I finished, I tucked the drawings into my closet so I could look at them every day while getting dressed, where the kids couldn't mess with them. The kids enjoyed the morning with their gifts. A little after 1 pm, I made them clean up and get ready to go to Jack's house for dinner, and Aaron came to pick Matt up.

Our Lyft driver pulled up in front of Jack's house, and we arrived on time. He had a beautiful home, decorated for Christmas, with a large yard. Luke asked, "Is he the President? This looks like the White House!" I laughed. "No, Luke, this house is a little smaller than the White House. It's big, but not that big." We rang the doorbell, and Jack opened it with a big smile. "Merry Christmas, Merry Christmas! Come on in and join the fun!"

The entryway was spacious, with a formal library warmed by a fireplace on one side and a large formal dining room on the other. In the center, a half-spiral staircase led to the second-floor balcony. A floating Castle Raindrop crystal chandelier illuminated the space. As we moved toward the back of the house, it opened to a large kitchen with an island bar on one side and a spacious family room on the other. In the corner of the family room, a 10-foot Christmas tree stood tall, surrounded by both opened and unopened presents. Christmas music played softly in the background while a football game aired on the 80-inch TV. Bowls of candy, platters of cookies, appetizers, and a beverage table offered every kind of drink imaginable. The kids must have thought they had died and gone to heaven.

Three women were in the kitchen preparing food. Jack's wife, Julia, was one of them and she immediately smiled and came over to greet us. She hugged each of us and welcomed us to her home. She treated each of the kids as if she had known them all their lives, talking with them excitedly about their Christmas morning visit from Santa. Lydia was especially delighted to get this kind of attention.

Jack then introduced me to his brother Maurice and his wife Stephanie. It was clear that Jack and Maurice resembled each other, though Maurice looked more like Harrison Ford, with blondish-grey ruffled hair. Jack's two grown sons, Zach and Rick, were so similar in appearance that they could have been twins, though they were 14 months apart. They resembled Ryan Reynolds, both tall, slender, and blonde, with soft features. Zach was married to Patricia, and they had two kids the same age as Lydia and Luke—Zach Jr. and Jacob. Rick, not married, was leaving to have dinner with his girlfriend and her family.

Maurice had two grown daughters, Tabitha and Monica, both in their mid-20s. Tabitha had dark hair and hazel eyes and was single, while Monica, with blonde hair like mine, was married to Bill. They had a one-year-old son named George. Zach Jr., being the oldest, asked Sara if they wanted to go play games, and the kids immediately dashed off to the playroom.

I asked Julia how I could help, and she said, "Everything's done, and we're ready to eat. Let's head to the dining room." I didn't think there was a table big enough to seat everyone, but Jack and Julia had a table that fit 12. Not only did it seat everyone, but it was loaded with turkey, ham, and a multitude of sides. The children were seated at a smaller table in an adjacent room where I could keep an eye on them to make sure they behaved.

Jack blessed the food with a heartfelt prayer of gratitude, and we dug in. Everything was so delicious that I overate, but when dessert came out, I found room for cheesecake.

Maurice asked where I was from. I explained that I'd moved around a lot, but I was born in Springfield, Massachusctts, where my mom had lived while attending Springfield College. Maurice smiled and said, "Isn't that a coincidence? I went to Springfield College too. Maybe I knew your mother. What year was she there?"

"Her name is Jane McInnis, she would have graduated with the class of 1994," I said.

Maurice paused, chewing a little slower as his expression shifted. "That's strange. I did know your mother. We hung out from time to time. How is she?" "She's fine," I said, not wanting to delve into why we weren't speaking at the dinner table. "Tell her I said hello the next time you talk to her."

The table grew quiet, and I began to feel uneasy until the doorbell rang. I remembered Jack mentioning that his brother had been in a car accident in college, almost dying. That must be why everyone had stopped talking.

Jack walked back in with Mike. Jack had invited him to come by after dinner with his mother. He'd invited his mother as well, but she had declined. It was good to see Mike. It felt like the cavalry had arrived. Mike immediately came over to me, possibly feeling some tension in the air, and gave me a hug and kiss on the cheek. Jack announced that it was game time, and he was ready to take on all challengers.

We all got up from the table and headed to the living room. Sara and I asked if we could help with the clean-up, and we were quickly put to work with the other women. It was nice being with the older women. I could feel that gentle, motherly energy in the air—a warmth I hadn't felt in a long time. When the kitchen was clean, we joined the others and played some family games, which were more for the kids than anything else.

Maurice approached me as I went to get another cup of egg-nog and said, "I didn't know your mother had married while she was in Springfield. Who is the lucky guy?" I told him that my mother didn't get married, and she told me very little about her time in Springfield.

"Who is your father?" Maurice asked. "I don't mean to pry but your mother left without a trace," I told Maurice that my mother told me my father died in a car crash, other than that I didn't know much about my father. My mother called him Moe. She never wanted to talk about him.

"In college, all my friends called me Moe. I was involved in a major car crash and died for a few minutes. They brought me back in the ambulance. I was in a coma for almost a month and had to leave school for the rest of the term to rehabilitate. When I was finally able to function on my own, I tried to find your mother. I never knew what happened to her or why she left. We had some great times, and I cared about her. I was considering asking her to marry me when we graduated. If you don't mind my asking, when is your birthday?" I told him, and he said, "This may sound strange to you, but I could very well be your father. I'm not sure if you've noticed the resemblance between you and my daughter, Monica. Jack talks about you all the time and how much you look like her. Would you consider getting a DNA test?"

This was way too much. How was all of this happening in such a short time span? How could I meet up with my father and reconnect with my son's father all in the same year? I had been living in this town with the same people for years without ever having run into any of them and within a matter of months it all changed. Why, how? Who could so perfectly orchestrate this? It was like something out of a Hallmark movie. "I must be dreaming," I muttered to myself and then it dawned on me in the dream this was leading to that life I said I wanted. This was leading me to all the parts of a life of true bliss.

" It's a lot to ask, but would you be willing to be tested?" Maurice asked. "Sure," I said. "Great. I'll make all the arrangements and get back to you, but we had better get back in there before we are missed."

We joined the others, but my mind was no longer in the same room, I was still dizzy with the thought that this was my family and Jack, who I had spent so much time talking to over the past year, was my uncle. It was all coming together better than I ever thought it could or should. I had a family. I was no longer alone.

Chapter 24

God answers our prayers not because we are good, but because He is good.
—Aiden Wilson Tozer

As Mike drove us home, I shared my conversation with Maurice. He was floored. "Now that you mention it, there is a strong resemblance between you and Maurice's daughter, Monica. This is incredible. You couldn't have asked for a better father than Maurice. I'm so happy for you; I know they will welcome you with open arms."

"Hey, I know you're leaving for Disney World tomorrow, but would you be willing to celebrate New Year's Eve with my mother and me?" I asked. "My mother loves preparing a big dinner for New Year's Eve, and I'd love for her to meet you and the kids. I want to start the first moments of the New Year with our families getting to know each other." "That would be great," I said.

With Mike's help, we brought all the presents upstairs and settled the kids before he pulled me into the hallway for a quick kiss goodnight. "I'm going to miss you," Mike said. "Hurry back!"

The next day, Ray and Eileen arrived as promised and shared the news with the kids. "We're going to Disney World!" They were ecstatic. Lydia cried tears of joy. "Go put on one of your new outfits from Christmas," I told them. I had secretly bought a couple of carry-on bags and new clothes for the kids for the trip. Eileen had the bags in the back of Ray's SUV. Eileen dropped us off at the airport, and we were on the plane bound for Orlando by noon. I could see the difference in Ray. The weakness in his arms was more noticeable now, and there was a slight limp. He used wheelchair assistance at the airport. Atlanta's airport was huge, and it was the first time the kids and I had ever flown anywhere. Their eyes were wide with excitement as they took everything in. On the plane, we sat together in two rows. I was with Luke and Lydia, and Ray was with Matt and Sara. Luke stayed glued to the window, fascinated by the plane's takeoff. I was nervous about flying but didn't want the kids to know.

When we arrived at the hotel, I saw that Ray had gone all out. We had two adjoining suites at the Walt Disney World Swan and Dolphin Resort. Ray had purchased special "Lightning" tickets, which allowed the kids to bypass regular lines. We went to four different parks and rode as many rides as we could. The kids loved the nightly fireworks, which we watched both in the park and from our hotel balcony. Ray took us out to dinner every night at a different restaurant. He bought the kids toys and souvenirs. He must have spent a fortune on this trip.

On our last night, after the kids went to bed, we sat quietly on the balcony of our hotel suite.

"Ruth, I have a few more trips in me, then I'll check into an assisted living center. I'm not going back to my house, and I want you to have it. I have enough money to get through to the end, and I can't take it with me. You've been like the daughter I always wanted, and I want you to have this house for you and the kids. The only condition is that you take it as-is; I won't clean it out. But it comes fully furnished. I've already put the deed in your name. It's yours, free and clear." "Ray, I don't know what to say. You've been so good to us. Thank you," I said, tears streaming down my face. I threw my arms around him, knowing he wouldn't let me be emotional for long. "Alright, enough of that. Time for me to turn in. I'm off to Dubai in two days," Ray grumbled. "Eileen and I have a flight leaving at 6:30 p.m. It's one of those fancy pods that turn into a bed, so I can rest and recover from Disney," he chuckled.

The day we returned from Disney, Eileen picked us up, and we went straight to Ray's house. He wanted to be the one to tell the kids that this was their new home. They couldn't believe it. It was a beautiful house in Grant Park with a small yard. "Oh, you can have my car too. I can't drive anymore," Ray said. He drove a late-model Ford Explorer, perfect for hauling the kids around. "Use it to bring your stuff over after I leave tomorrow. Go ahead and take it now. We have a limo picking us up tomorrow."

When we arrived back at our apartment, the first thing we noticed was that someone had been inside. Nothing significant had been taken, but some items had been moved, and a few things were missing, nothing major. It felt unsettling, and we all felt uncomfortable. The lock hadn't been broken, and nothing valuable was gone, so I didn't feel right reporting it to the police. What could they do, anyway? "Pack your things," I said to the kids. "This is a sign. We're moving to Uncle Ray's tomorrow."

Mike came over as soon as I told him what happened. I needed to tell someone. The kids excitedly shared everything about their Disney trip, showing him their souvenirs. Mike ordered pizza, and we played games with Lydia and Luke, while Matt went out with his father to shoot hoops, and Sara read The Lord of the Rings in her room—a Christmas gift. The evening was so wonderful that I didn't want it to end. I could tell Mike felt the same way, but I insisted he go home. We walked down the stairs to his car, savoring those last few minutes together. Mike held my hand, and as he turned to embrace me, the hooded guy suddenly appeared from a dark corner and tackled Mike to the ground. "She's mine! I saw her first! You can't have her, Mike! She's mine!" the man screamed. I finally grasped who the hooded guy was—Slimy Simon. It didn't take long for Mike to overpower him and pin him down. "Simon, stop it!" Mike ordered. "Calm down, or I'll call the police." Simon stopped struggling, and Mike released him. "I've been looking for you everywhere. Where have you been?" Mike asked. "I've been protecting the light. She's the lady of light. She brings calm. She makes me feel alright. You can't have her. I need her! I need her!" Simon began to get agitated all over again. I took a deep breath, trying to focus. "Simon, the light is in you too. You don't need me to see it or have it," I said softly. "You're not at the diner anymore. I can only see you by standing out here," Simon said, a little calmer now.

You can come see me anytime you want; you don't have to stand outside and wait." "I can?" Simon asked. Yes, you can! Simon, I'm going to meet your mother tomorrow. Do you want to come with me?" "No, no, no, no, no, no, no, no, the mean man is there, and I can't see him, no!" Simon said. "He's not there anymore Simon," Mike said. "It's just me and Mom. She would be so happy to see you, Simon. Please come with us." Simon looked from me to Mike and back to me before saying, "Okay, I'll come." With that, he turned and walked away into the shadows of the street.

"I'm so sorry Ruth," Mike said. "I had no idea he was hanging around here. I never put the pieces together, even after you told me he came to the restaurant every day." "It's okay Mike it's okay. I think I can help him, I said. "Ruth, I don't know about that, I've never seen him so agitated and violent," Mike said. "I see something familiar in him, something I can connect with. I know where he is and how to bring him out. Trust me, it will be okay. Let's talk about it some more tomorrow. I'm looking forward to meeting your mother and she is going to be so happy to see Simon." I said. "That's if he shows up," Mike said. "Oh, he will, I'm sure of it. Good night, Mike!" I said. "Flip the switch when you get upstairs, please," Mike asked. I kissed him on the cheek and walked into the apartment building's lobby.

Chapter 25

"People come into your life for a reason, a season, or a lifetime."
—Brian Chalker

New Year's Eve! That was my first thought when I woke up. It had been an amazing year, and I truly believed the next year would be even better. I was overjoyed as I went through my gratitude list. After a prayer of thanks, I took some time to meditate.

The kids had spent most of the evening packing. I only had a few more things left to box up. We hadn't planned on taking any furniture since there was nowhere to put it at Ray's house. It was all junk anyway and probably would have fallen apart during the move. After just two trips, everything was out of the apartment and over at Ray's. We returned one last time for a final walk-through, standing in the quiet to say goodbye before closing the door on this chapter of our lives. When we got downstairs, a man was standing on the sidewalk facing the street. He turned around, and I was surprised to see it was Simon.

He was all cleaned up — hair washed, freshly shaved, and dressed in nice clothes. I barely recognized him. I smiled with giddy enthusiasm, and Simon returned a small smile. "Shall we?" I said, opening the door for him to get in the car.

"Mom, who is this?" Matt asked.

"This is Simon Bradford, Mike's brother. He's coming with us to dinner at his mother's house." All four kids were stunned into silence — even Sara, who's always talking, had nothing to say. We drove in silence for a little while until I turned on the radio. It was a station that played music from the 80s. Simon started singing along, and I joined him. Before long, everyone was singing.

Mike and his mother lived in Buckhead, an affluent part of Atlanta. I hadn't been to Mike's house before, nor had I ever driven through that neighborhood. The kids and I were amazed at the size of the houses. When we finally reached the address Mike had given us, the car fell completely silent. We drove down a long, winding driveway and parked in front of the house.

Mike bounded out the door before we could even get out of the car, visibly excited and emotional at the sight of Simon. He ushered us inside, and a beautiful woman came around the corner — her eyes immediately filling with tears of joy. She ran to Simon and held him in a tight embrace for several minutes. Finally, she looked up at me. We both smiled with recognition and embraced wordlessly. "Hi Gladys, it's so good to see you," I said. "Ruth, I had no idea you were the woman my son has been talking my ear off about!" she said, laughing through her tears. "Wait a minute," Mike interrupted. "How do you two know each other?" "Ruth helped me out one day when I ran out of gas around the corner from the diner," Gladys explained. "I was down there driving around, hoping I might catch a glimpse of Simon. And now, she's brought my son home."

****

Christian's mission was officially complete. He had set Ruth on the Path to True Bliss. He would still check in on her from time to time, but now, there were others to walk alongside her every day. Though she would continue to face challenges and endure disappointment, she now had everything she needed to weather even the roughest storms.

Epilogue

Jane walked out of the prison gates and looked up at the sky, seeing it for the first time as a free woman in fifteen years. Prison had been both the best and worst thing that had ever happened to her. She had been arrested for manslaughter after a late-night accident, caused by her drinking, took the life of her lover. Prison had sobered her up. It had forced her to stop running from her past. Coming to terms with the devastation alcohol had wreaked on her life hadn't been easy, but she had done the hard work. Now, it was time to make amends — the next step in her twelve-step program. First on her list was her daughter, Ruth, who might not want anything to do with her. Jane knew she had been a terrible mother. If Ruth turned her back on her, Jane wouldn't blame her. But she would find her, and she would offer a sincere apology. Second on her list was visiting Maurice's family. They deserved to know the truth: Jane had been the driver that night. She had done everything she could to save him. After the accident, she had sprinted down the street to a phone booth to call 911. By the time she returned, ambulances were already at the scene. She overheard the EMTs saying he no longer had a pulse. Jane had spent years trying to drown the guilt and pain of losing Moe. Now, at least, she could tell his family that a part of him lived on — in his daughter.

Made in the USA
Columbia, SC
08 June 2025